LOW KEY FALLIN' FOR A SAVAGE 3

J. DOMINIQUE

Cole Hart
SIGNATURE NOVELS

Low Key Fallin' For A Savage 3

Copyright © 2020 by J. Dominique

All rights reserved.

Published in the United States of America.

Published by Cole Hart Signature, LLC.

Mailing List

To stay up to date on new releases, plus get information on contests, sneak peeks, and more,

Go To The Website Below...

www.colehartsignature.com

JUICE

I was ready to kill Destiny's bitch ass baby daddy after finding out what he did, but I was already being watched by the police while they did this fuck ass investigation, so I had to let him be. When she'd told me what happened at the school and why, I was fuming. The whole time I'd known their asses, I'd never seen that nigga and now all of a sudden, he wanted to try and take Yo'Sahn away. I was pissed off even more when she told me that he'd come up to the hospital trying to speak on my presence in shorty's life, when he hadn't even been there. That nigga was begging for me to come see him, but I needed to clear me and Destiny's names first.

Today was the day that we had to meet with the detectives, and no matter how much I tried to reassure her, Destiny was nervous as hell. I squeezed her hand before bringing it to my lips as we pulled up in front of the police station.

"You cool, cause we can do this shit another day if you want," I asked, dead serious.

If she told me that she wanted to go home, then I'd pull clean off and tell Smith to pick another day. She was already going through a bunch of shit and this was only adding stress to the situation. Sighing, she shook her head and looked up at the building with her lip turned up.

"Nah, we might as well get it over with." She shrugged, not knowing how sexy her strength was to me. I always bragged on what type of mother she was and how she got shit done, because I loved how strong she was. All this time, I'd been chasing pretty ass bird brained bitches, but Destiny had brains and beauty. She was nothing like any of the hoes I'd had in the past, in fact, she was reminding me of my OG more and more.

"Aight, cool, here come Smith now." I spotted him a few cars ahead, making his way towards us in an expensive ass suit like we were going to court or some shit. Destiny had tried to dress up too, and I shut her straight down. Wasn't no way I was gone let her walk up in there in a pencil skirt, trying to suffocate my baby. I snatched her up some joggers just like I was wearing and a t-shirt. There was no telling how long they'd try to question us, and I wanted her to be comfortable and warm since it was always cold as fuck in them interrogation rooms.

We both stepped out at the same time and met him on the curb as he grinned widely, showing all thirty-two teeth at Destiny. I swear, he wanted me to go across his shit.

"As always, it's a pleasure seeing you, Destiny," he simpered, reaching for her hand and I quickly grabbed it up in my own, intertwining my fingers with hers.

"You keep trying me, Smith, and I'm gone break your shit," I told him, causing his grin to drop completely from his face. He straightened his tie and cleared his throat uncomfortably, but I hoped that he'd heed my warning. That flirting shit was probably cute to his other clients, but I didn't play that shit.

"Sorry." Taking a step back, he put his focus on me, making sure not to even look Destiny's way. "I talked to both Detective Jones and Detective Brown and told them that I'll be sitting in on both interrogations. So, one of you will be waiting while the other is questioned if that's okay with you," his question was directed at me, but Destiny was the one that spoke up.

"Wait, waiting in here?" her displeasure was evident on her face as she pointed up at the building.

"You can go first, and I'll wait, and you can just leave when you done." I wasn't pressed about being there. Regardless of what they thought they had, which I knew to only be the coincidence of Ms. Taylor dying after her report, that wasn't shit to me. I hadn't left any evidence, and I hadn't told Destiny shit about what I'd done, so they had less than nothing. Nodding, she accepted my offer to go first, mumbling an okay.

I walked in with her and Smith, giving her a quick kiss before they were escorted away by one of the lazy ass police that sat behind the desk. As soon as they disappeared around the corner, I dipped back to the car. Wasn't no way I was going to be sitting in there with all of them staring at me all crazy and shit. I wanted to flame up, but I wasn't stupid enough to do it right outside of the police station, so instead, I grabbed one of the edible rice crispy treats I had stashed.

Thirty minutes later, I'd swallowed three more and was listening to J. Cole's latest joint, high as fuck. I had my seat laid damn near all the way back and my hat pulled down over my eyes, dozing off when my phone rang. I really ain't want to answer that shit, but with the way things were going, I couldn't afford not to.

Seeing that it was Eazy, I didn't hesitate to answer. "What's up, bruh?"

"Shit, just made it down to the club, I was just making sure y'all was cool. I know you had to do that thing, today," he said, referring to us being questioned by the detectives.

When he'd told me about them coming to the club and harassing him, I was highly irritated. It wasn't like it was out of the norm for them to stalk a nigga whole family, but I didn't see the point. If anything, they were damaging their own case on some goofy shit, and I had to wonder who had allowed them to become detectives in the first place.

"We just got here not too long ago. Smith and Destiny went in first *though, since she all nervous and shit," I let him know, absentmindedly while looking out at the cars driving past.*

"Them muhfuckas ain't got shit, she gone be cool."

"I already know, I done told her slow ass, but you know her and Dream ain't used to this type of shit." I sighed and ran a hand down my face. If they were just wanting me, then I wouldn't even care because I know how they do, but since they were coming after Destiny too, it was different. Especially, since she was pregnant. Behind my child though, I'd blow this whole precinct up, so it was in their best interest to not stress her out.

"Facts but let me call you back, bruh, these fuckin construction niggas don't know what the fuck they doin!"

Before I could even respond, his rude ass had already hung up. He was a bitch for that, but I was too high to even trip. Besides that, I was getting restless as hell just sitting in the car waiting. Realizing that I hadn't talked to my pops in a few days, I dialed his number hoping to check up on him. He hadn't been himself since my OG passed, but he'd been hanging in there. Shit, the first couple days, I ain't even want to eat, but Destiny was on my ass. That just reminded me of what he was missing, not having his backbone there. After all this shit died down, I'd have to make sure that I looked out because we were all he had anymore.

"What yo ass want, Jeremiah!" he huffed as soon as he answered.

"Man, yo old ass sound just like Eazy." I chuckled, sucking my teeth. "I'm just tryna see how you doin, and you talkin crazy."

"Maybe, I sound like him cause you get on both our nerves, lil nigga." He joined in my laughter, and it felt good to hear him not sounding as down as he had the last few times we'd talked. "I'm cool though, man, watching some game highlights and drinking a beer."

"That's what's up. I was gone come see you and bring Yo'Sahn with me after I take care of this lil business."

"Uhhh, sounds like a plan, just-just call when you on the way." I didn't miss the hesitation in his voice, but I wasn't going to let that stop me from going to see him.

"*Bet, I might can get Eazy to bring his ass too. Hold up, this him right here.*" *I accepted Eazy's call, putting us on three-way.* "*Aye, pops on the line bro—*"

Boom! Boom! Rattattatat!

Gunfire erupted through the phone, instantly stopping my heart. "*Eazy! Aye Eazy!*" *me and my pops continued to yell his name as grunting filled our ears.*

"*Elijah! Jeremiah, if this a joke this shit ain't funny, nigga!*" *my pops went off.*

"*It ain't! I'm on my way to him now!*" *I barked, jumping in the driver's seat.*

Tossing the phone, I pulled off weaving in and out of traffic; cursing out loud as I realized I'd left my gun at home. This was not the time for this shit! I can't even lie, tears were stinging my eyes as I defied the speed limit, trying to get to my brother. Horns were blowing, and people were cursing me out from the Grand Theft Auto type of driving that I was doing. I'd nearly gotten into at least three accidents by the time I'd actually made it to his club. I slammed the car in park and jumped out and ran into the building. I was ready for whatever—gun or no gun—and damn near dropped to my knees at the sight of the massacre on the first floor. It looked like at least twenty construction workers scattered across the floor and covered in blood. They obviously hadn't been expecting whatever had gone down.

"*ELIJAH!*" *I shouted his name as I made my way through the bodies and to the stairs that led to his office. The longer I went without hearing anything, the more my heart pounded in my chest.* "*ELIJ-ah, fuck bro!*" *my voice cracked as soon as I made it to his door and saw him sprawled out on the floor next to his desk, with his shirt drenched in blood. Rushing to his side, I lifted him into my arms as the tears I'd been trying to hold on to, finally spilled out across his face.*

"*Ju-Juice,*" *blood gushed from his mouth as he struggled to speak, looking at me with wide, terror-stricken eyes.*

"*Don't try and talk, man, I got you. Stay with me, bro aight, stay* with me." I could barely get out anything coherent between being over-whelmed with emotion and trying to search for my phone.

I quickly realized that I'd left it in the car and angrily clenched my teeth so hard, I thought they'd break. Frantically, I searched for his phone or at the very least his office phone, so I could dial 911, and my eyes fell on another body in the room. Further inspection revealed that it was Dre. Half of his face was blown off and covered in blood, but there was no mistaking who it was. I knew right then that he'd come in busting, and Eazy had delivered him a fatal shot after taking multiple rounds. Even though that nigga was clearly dead, I still wanted to pick up the AK he had lying beside him and shoot until his head was completely gone but getting Eazy to the hospital was more important. It was hard to tear my eyes away from his scum ass, but I managed to, and a second later, I found the phone lying right up under the desk. After calling 911 and alerting them of what happened, I continued to talk to my brother, even as his breathing grew hollow and shaky. Then I did some shit I hadn't done since I was a little ass kid... I prayed.

An hour later, I was still praying as we waited in the emergency room for a doctor to come and tell us something. My pops was slumped over in a chair in the corner with his face buried in his hands, and I knew it was to hide his tears. Once again, he was trying to be strong, but I knew that shit was hard on him. Destiny had called shortly after we'd gotten there and ended up telling me she was done with her inter-view, but I'd forgotten all about that shit. I told Smith to tell them fuck ass detectives that I would reschedule when I could because my focus was on my brother at the moment, and I didn't give a fuck how they felt about it. I tried to get him to give Destiny a ride home, but she'd insisted on coming, so she sat next to my dad and tried to comfort him even though I knew she was fucked up too. In addition to what she had to deal with earlier, I'm sure this situation was like déjà vu to her. She met my eyes and gave me a reassuring smile, but I wasn't even in the headspace to return it. I needed to know something, and I was damn near ready to take off to the back myself. Releasing a long and irritated sigh, I finally took a seat and tried to get my emotions under control, but the shit wasn't working. My eyes landed on the door and was surprised to see a face I wasn't expecting. He walked right over to where we were, and I stood up to meet him.

"Pierre, what you doin up here?" I asked, confused about seeing our connect. As far as we both knew, he stayed out in New York, so it was weird to see him there. In all the years we'd worked with him, he only came down when it was time for a meeting. Pierre didn't even come up for shipments, so this shit was throwing me for a loop.

"I was in the area and heard about what happened to Elijah, so I stopped by. Is there anything I can do or get to help?" That shit had me squinting at him suspiciously, but when my pops' head shot up and hate filled his face, I knew it was about to be some shit.

"What the fuck are you doin here, nigga!" he roared, shrugging Destiny's hand away and jumping in Pierre's face.

"What you think, Elijah? Rachel's dead now, ain't no more lying about the shit!"

I looked back and forth between the two as they faced off, trying to figure out what the fuck was going on. How they even knew each other was beyond me.

"Nigga, don't speak my wife's name!" my pops thundered.

"I know one of y'all better tell me what the fuck going on!" They continued to stare each other down without speaking while I waited, growing more and more pissed off.

"You gone tell him or you want me to?" Pierre questioned, barely moving his lips as he spoke. This entire time, he seemed more composed than my pops; the more he talked, the angrier my old man got. Before he could answer, the doctor came out and called for family members to step forward. For the moment, the conversation was paused, but as soon as I got word on my brother, we were going to get to the bottom of this shit.

"Well, Elijah is strong. He suffered a total of six wounds—three in the abdomen, one in the leg and two through and through in the arm.

JUICE

He did suffer a collapsed lung, but we were able to stabilize him. Now, he will need a blood transfusion, is anybody willing to be tested?" the doctor said as a matter of fact, looking at each of us.

"No need to test, I'm his father," Pierre said, shocking us all.

BUDDA

I still had yet to hear back from Dre, after I'd sent him on that dummy mission earlier, but that had been the point. My hope was that his slow ass would go in and get himself killed more than anything, at this point. I was tired of supporting his bum ass! He was more of a drain than anything, and if what I had planned was going to work, then I needed to limit the people involved. Did I want to kill Juice and Eazy? Hell yeah, but them niggas had nine lives or some shit, and it was way harder to find anybody to get on my team than I thought it would be. At this point, I was a one-man army, besides Olivia, and I planned to use her ass too if I could.

"What are we doin here, Budda, damn!" Olivia whined from the passenger seat, irritating me instantly.

"Don't ask me no fuckin questions! We gone do what I say, when I say it!" As soon as I raised my voice, she winced, only infuriating me more. She was acting as if I hadn't walked her through this entire thing already, but that was the way she tweaked. Yeah, you read that right, she was snorting coke and lacing blunts right along with me now. After that last ass whooping, I'd put on her, she'd let me get her hooked on the very drug she claimed to despise. Us getting put out after I'd tricked off the rent money helped in making her depend on it even

more. *Her being addicted helped me have even more control over her, but at the same time, it made her jumpy as fuck which often pissed me off. The plan had been to send Dre off to try and kill Eazy, and while they were distracted killing or torturing him, me and Olivia would rob Trell after he did his pick-ups. It would be one of the easiest licks I'd ever hit, and it was literally idiot-proof, which is why I didn't mind having her with me. Two heads are better than one, even if one of them was lacking common sense. Besides, I needed a driver while I did the snatch and grab. I didn't trust that her stupid ass wouldn't fuck something up, then I'd surely have to kill her, and I really didn't want to do that just yet. If it wasn't for her constant yapping, I would've never run into Trell in the first place. One of the many nights that I'd taken her car and gone out on the hunt for more drugs, I'd peeped him leaving the known trap with a duffle bag. I played it cool and followed him back to his house. It took a week of me following him around for me to get his schedule down and when I did, I realized that he was doing the pick-ups for Juice and Eazy. That opened up a whole new possibility for me; I could literally kill two birds with one stone. If I stole their money, I could fuck them up and get back on since Santos had no intentions of loaning me shit.*

So, now we were sitting almost a block away from the trap, waiting on Trell to come out with the last bag of the day. I figured I may as well do it big and snatch up everything I could at once. Not too long later, I saw him bopping down the front steps, and I quickly tapped Olivia on the arm.

"Aye, follow that car." Of course, she couldn't do so without rolling her eyes and smacking those fat ass lips. *I had to restrain myself from smashing her face through the window because I knew if I did, she wouldn't be able to drive anymore. Weak ass bitch would probably pass out, then I'd be on my own, and I couldn't afford that.*

"Just do what the fuck I said!" I barked, forcing her to jerk out into the street. *"Bitch, I swear if you fuck this up for me, I'm gone beat yo ass! Now, go!"* I was damn near foaming at the mouth dealing with this silly bitch, but thankfully, she got her shit together and began

following him from a safe distance. After all of this time, I knew that he was headed to his house to do the count and then he'd take the money to Juice, like his little bitch or something. So, the closer we got to his place, I had Olivia speed up.

"Go, go, go!"

She pressed the gas harder and pulled up alongside him with fear and anxiety covering her face. That didn't stop me from jerking the wheel towards his car and slamming right into the side of it.

"Ahhhh, what the fuck Budda!" she shrieked loudly, clutching her face like the kid from Home Alone. Still holding onto the wheel, myself, I pulled my gun out.

"Put yo gah damn hands back, stupid!" I spat, turning my attention back to where Trell was attempting to get away.

He seemed like he was struggling to pull out his own weapon, and I wasn't about to let him shoot me. As soon as I knew that Olivia had control of the wheel, I fired three rounds out of the open window, instantly shattering the glass on his car and hitting him in the neck. His car fishtailed and veered right off the road, and I pointed for her to follow. By the time, her dumb ass finally pulled over and I got out, I could see Trell trying to crawl away. The look on his face when he saw me was priceless, but not more than what he had in his trunk. Without thinking, I raised my gun and shot him in the back of the head, dropping him right on the grassy hill he'd made it to. After making sure he was dead, I grabbed each of the six bags and placed them in her car, before jumping back in.

"Get us up outta here now!"

She was pulling off before I'd barely had the words out of my mouth, but it was necessary because it was already people out trying to pull over and help. Little did they know that nigga was dead, and he wasn't comin back...

To be continued...

———

JUICE

*I*magine thinking that your day couldn't get any worse and then boom, it does, and you get some straight life-altering news. Pierre had just fucked-up my entire life with the shit he'd said. I was ready to shoot his old ass right there in the ER for even disrespecting my pops like that, but one look at my old man, and I knew what he'd said was true! Pierre was Eazy's daddy!

"Nah! *I'm* his father! You ain't shit but a donor muhfucka!" my pops sneered, pounding his chest while the doctor looked between the two uncomfortably.

"And why is that, huh? You think I wanted to walk away, nigga!" Pierre seemed unbothered by our pops' rage, that much was evident in the way he didn't back down.

"Yo pops, what the fuck this nigga talkin bout?" I demanded, deciding to address my father and not our business partner, despite him being the one that caused this confusion. When Elijah King Sr. looked my way, I could see the disappointment in his eyes, but before he could speak, the doctor cleared his throat once again.

"Uhhh, gentleman, we really need to get this done before Elijah's condition worsens."

"Exactly!" Pierre jumped in. "You're wasting precious time when you know the truth already. Now if you're done, I'd like to go back and save *my son.*" His snide tone had my pops snatching him up by his collar, unfazed by the two goons he'd walked in with, suddenly starting to approach. Pierre quickly held up a hand to stop them, seeming more amused than anything.

"The only reason yo ass is getting a pass right now is because of that boy back there, but don't get shit twisted. He can still get that blood whether you're alive or not! Nigga, don't forget I'm still *that* nigga!"

Scoffing, my pops shoved him away as I tried to mentally take in what had just happened. He walked off, making sure to shoulder check the two bodyguards on his way out the emergency room doors, while Pierre merely straightened his suit and allowed the shaken doctor to lead him to the back.

I hadn't realized that I was still standing there stuck until I felt Destiny beside me, looking up at me with sad eyes. "Are you okay, babe?"

"I need to go talk to my pops," was all I said before trudging away, feeling weighed down. I didn't mean to seem so cold with her, but the truth is, we'd been taking massive losses lately. Now with my brother back there fighting for his life, I was hit with the shocking news that our dad wasn't who we thought he was. The shit truthfully had me fucked up mentally. It seemed like too much was being thrown at me at once, and I wasn't the brother that thought shit through before acting. I was the one that handled things with my fist or guns, but this emotional ass shit right here? What the fuck was I supposed to do with this?

I found my pops sitting outside on the bricks with his head down and a burning square in his hand, something that surprised the fuck out of me. As far as I knew, he'd stopped smoking years ago at the behest of my OG, who wasn't tolerating that shit, so my face instantly frowned up. Despite how loud the city was, it seemed like he heard me coming because he turned and looked my way as I got closer.

"When you start smoking again, old man?" I asked the question that seemed the least confrontational at the moment, causing him to chuckle bitterly.

"I started back the same day as yo mama funeral, but that ain't really what you wanna know, is it?" He took one last pull off his cigarette and then mashed it out in the grass as I took a seat beside him.

"Jus—just tell me what the fuck goin on?" I couldn't even force myself to say the words out loud as I timidly looked at my father.

This shit had me feeling so out of touch with myself that I wasn't even being the normal Juice. Being timid or afraid just weren't feelings that I normally had, but they'd both been prevalent for the last couple months as shit after shit kept coming my way. Like right at this moment, my heart was pounding just knowing that my pops wasn't going to be able to dismiss what Pierre had said. At this point, it was just a matter of *what* had happened.

"Look, I never told y'all that when I met yo mother, she was already in a situation with that nigga," he spat, nodding back towards the hospital. "She was young and fascinated with the lifestyle he lived, so it was easy for him to bag her, but what he wasn't expecting was that she didn't fit in that world. I recognized it right away and instead of backing off, I stayed on her. I didn't let up at all, and it didn't help that Pierre had a few uh, *problems* of his own that aided in their shit ending. It wasn't long before he'd messed-up, cheating and endangering her life again. She came to me, sometime after we got together, then she found out that she was pregnant with Elijah. We didn't know that he was Pierre's until her first appointment, when they told us exactly how far along she was. Being the man I am, I was prepared from jump to do what needed to be done. Rachel allowed me to step in; we even named him after me, but Pierre saw her out with him one day when he was about three and knew right away Elijah was his. He took him from her that day, and she came home in tears." He shook his head at the memory while I sat taking everything in.

"Now you don't know this but, yo pops ain't always been so ummm *law abiding*. I did my lil dirt, but it was nowhere near on the same scale as Pierre. It's nothing I'm proud of, but I own my shit... anyway, when yo mama told me what happened, I immediately stepped in. Had a few of my guys ready to storm that nigga's house and get *my son* back, but it seemed that God beat me to it. Before he could even make it home, someone had shot up the car he was in. Elijah got away with barely a scratch on him, but the shit scared Pierre so bad that he brought him back and promised to stay away, so that he'd be safe. I guess that shit was contingent on Rachel being alive."

It was clear my pops still had a deep disdain for this nigga, and I could understand why, considering everything that had gone on in their past. He'd just dropped a lot on me, and I was still stuck on the crazy ass love triangle they had going on. To know that all this time, Pierre had been working with us knowing that he was Eazy's father was some straight soap opera shit.

"Damn, I don't even know what to say, this shit is nuts, man."

"You don't have to say nothing. This doesn't change anything for me, never did and never will. I'm still y'all's old man," he said, placing a hand on my shoulder and looking me in the eyes. The look of uncertainty on his face bothered the fuck out of me because I felt the same way, regardless. There was no telling how Eazy would take the news, though, and that was probably what had him so down. Sensing that he needed it, I leaned over and gave him a hug.

"Juice! Ju—oh, my God!" Destiny's loud ass had us pulling

apart. I instantly tensed and stood as she ran over with tears streaming down her face.

"Stop running and shit! You probably got my baby bouncing around in there!" I snapped, shortening the distance between us with a few steps. She finally slowed down to a fast-paced walk, meeting me in the middle. "Now, what happened? Did they come back out?" I was already preparing to go back inside, but she gripped my arm, stopping me with a shake of her head.

"Somebody named Daren called... he said Trell got robbed and shot.... It's bad."

DREAM

I blew out an aggravated gust of air as I walked to my car, coming from yet another bank where I was rejected for a business loan. Despite being able to show the success we'd had with our business, the small timeframe spoke volumes more than anything else. They didn't care how well we'd done because we had only been doing so for roughly two months, not only that, but we clearly hadn't even made enough to save and put towards another building. And in the words of the banker, "We'd made ourselves look even worse by not having insurance in the first place."

This was only my second denial, but it wasn't any less devastating than the first. Tears were already running down my face in frustration, but I quickly sucked up my disappointment and got myself together when I saw my sister calling. I checked myself in the mirror like she was calling me on FaceTime and sniffled before sliding the icon across my screen.

"He—hey bitch, I—"

"Dream! I need you to pick up Yo'Sahn, drop him off at mama's, and get to University right now, it's an emergency!" Her voice was strained as she cut me off, instantly wiping the fake smile off my face. I knew whatever was wrong had to be serious for her to want Yoshi with our mama, considering, but her tone left no room for questioning. Without even knowing what was going on, a fresh set of tears filled my eyes.

"What happened, Destiny? Who's at the hospital!" I croaked as my heart damn near leapt out of my chest. There was a pregnant pause as if she was trying to consider her words before speaking letting me know it was even worse than I could imagine.

"It's… it's Eazy." Again, she went silent, probably waiting on my reaction, but I was too stunned to speak.

Not even a month had passed since Ms. Rachel's death, Juice and Yoshi were still recovering after getting shot, and now this? I didn't even know the extent of his injuries, but I was worried, nonetheless. The shit that had happened between us was now minor in comparison to him being laid up in the hospital, as worry had me starting up my car and whipping through the streets to get to the school.

"Dre came up to his club, and they had a shootout… he's dead, but Eazy is in critical condition. I know it's asking a lot for you to not be here right now, but some shit just went down, and I can't leave."

The more she talked, the more emotion I could hear through the phone, and I quickly reassured her that it was alright. She was already dealing with a lot and she was pregnant, so I didn't want her stressing about anything else.

"I'm going to the school now, but are you sure it's okay for me to drop him off over there?"

"Yeah, I already sent her a Cash App for it, so she should be waiting for y'all," she said, and I rolled my eyes at how ridiculous our mama was. I was sure that Destiny had told her what was going on, but of course, she didn't give a single fuck. All Adina was worried about was some damn money. I opted to keep my opinion of it to myself, but I was livid.

"Aight, I'll be there in a minute," I told her before hanging up and calling the school, so that they could have Yo'Sahn ready when I got there. The secretary assured me that she would have him pulled out of class and not too long after, I was pulling up out front. Before I could bring my car to a complete stop, he was walking out of the building with a mixture of confusion and fear on his face.

"What's up, TeTe, why you pickin me up so early?" was the first thing out of his mouth as he climbed into the car, and I realized that I hadn't been prepared for that question.

The worry in his eyes showed that he sensed something was wrong, and I hoped I wasn't giving anything away. Destiny hadn't said whether or not she wanted him to know what was going on, but I figured that she didn't, especially considering how much he'd already been through lately. There was no telling how he would take the news of Eazy being in the hospital, so I thought up a quick lie.

Plastering a fake smile on my face, I shrugged. "Me and your mom got some stuff to do, so I'm going to drop you to your grandma's for a little bit." I was hoping that he didn't notice the slight tremble in my voice as I drove away, focusing my attention on the street ahead. The mention of my mama instantly put him on high alert though. Not only had we rarely taken him there, but he was well aware of the strained relationship with her. I went to cut the radio up and tried to ignore the way he was squinting at me, in suspicion.

"My grandma….why I'm goin over there? She be trippin, you can just have Juice come get me or better yet, Eazy."

The mention of Elijah had my eyes stinging with tears yet again and the little bit of resolve I had, vanished. I really was trying my hardest not to let him know about Elijah's condition, especially since I didn't know shit other than that he had been shot and was in the hospital.

"Uhhh, they didn't answer the phone when I called," I lied quickly, nodding as if I was trying to convince myself too.

"They okay? Did somebody check to make sure they're straight cause they don't ever not answer the phone—let me just call em." He already had his phone out speed dialing before I could stop him. I knew neither Eazy nor Juice would answer anyway, so I didn't make a move to stop him. At least, I hoped Juice wouldn't. My prayers must have been heard because a second later, he groaned in frustration and slammed his phone down against the seat.

"See," my voice cracked, "they're busy or something.… Give them some time to handle whatever it is they're doin and try again," I told him, turning onto my mama's block. We both tensed the closer we got, not sure of how she was going to act.

"Well, I hope whatever they doin don't take no long ass time cause, grandma mean as hell," Yo'Sahn grumbled, slipping his bag back onto his shoulder as he got out.

I was so filled with guilt that I didn't even slap his little bad ass for cussing like I should have. Instead, I got out too and walked with him to her door, pressing the buzzer once we stopped inside the hallway.

"*What!*"

I rolled my eyes at her rude ass and released a heavy sigh. "Ma, I'm here to drop Yo'Sahn off."

"*Drop him off?* For how long, shit, because I got somethin to do, later?" she huffed, causing him to give me a knowing look. As bad as I wanted to curse her out again, I held it together, merely gritting my teeth instead.

"Destiny said she talked to you earlier.…and she said she paid you, ma, so quit playing and let him up."

"Fine, but y'all hoes bet not be taking all day!" her loud ass buzzer sounded, and I pulled the door open, silently pleading with Yo'Sahn to behave. The best way to deal with our mother was to ignore her, and with his phone, I was sure he wouldn't have any problems.

"It's only going to be for a little while, Yoshi, so just try and stay out of her way, and we'll be back before you know it." I gave him a reassuring smile even though he was clearly unhappy about the situation.

"Hurry yo lil ass up!" she shouted from the top of the stairs like she didn't live in a damn building and wasn't talking to her own grandson. Yo'Sahn sucked his teeth and went ahead inside, without saying anything else. The second he disappeared up the stairs, I blew out the breath that I hadn't realized I was holding and shot my ass back to my car.

When I finally made it to the hospital, I found Destiny pacing the waiting room floor while Mr. King sat behind her, glaring at another man across the room. Unsure of what was going on, I eased over to where she was staring at the two men in confusion.

"Dream! Oh, God, I'm so glad you're here!" She instantly grabbed me up into a tight embrace.

"What happened?" I asked when we separated. Destiny sniffled and prepared herself to speak, but a doctor came over and interrupted whatever it was she was about to say.

"Doc, what's the word?" the random man and Mr. King both approached the doctor at the same time, but he was the first to ask, causing Mr. King's face to ball up.

"Well, the transfusion went great, and Elijah is in stable condition. He's heavily sedated at the moment and is resting comfortably. If you all would like to go back and see, him he's in room 1208."

"Oh, thank God!" Destiny screamed while I gasped, unable to speak as a fresh wave of tears hit me. Despite everything that we'd been through, I was overjoyed that he was still alive and before anybody else could, I raced over to the double doors he'd just come through.

When I finally made it to Elijah's room, my heart was pounding against my chest, and I almost fell to my knees from weakness. He was almost unrecognizable with so many tubes and wires attached to him, but the fact that his chest was rising and falling was enough for me. I slowly made my way over to his side, grabbing his hand up in mine as everyone else filed into the room behind me. Destiny had her phone to her ear, speaking in a hushed tone while Mr. King and the other guy came to stand beside his bed also. The tension in the room was thick, and no one really spoke while the two men stared at each other angrily. I didn't know what the fuck was going on, but I'd just ask Destiny later. At the moment, my focus was on Elijah.

DESTINY

"*I* know you see me callin yo black ass, Jeremiah! You better call me back and let me know you're okay, or I swear to God..." my voice trailed off, and I chuckled angrily, really wanting to punch his ass in his shit.

Without another word, I hung up and prepared myself to get out of my car, so I could grab Yo'Sahn. I knew he was probably mad as hell about having to stay with my mama, but I really didn't have any choice. After the DCFS scare, I didn't want to have him at the hospital for God knows how long because of another shooting. Plus, he loved Eazy just like he loved Juice, and I knew that when he found out he'd be heartbroken.

I made it up to her door and hit the buzzer, preparing myself for her nasty attitude after leaving him there for so long. When she still hadn't come to answer a few minutes later, I pressed the buzzer again and pulled out my phone to call her ass at the same time. Today had been a stressful mess, and all I wanted to do was take a shower, lay down, and wait for Juice to bring his ass home.

"Who is it!" she came over the intercom, talking loud with attitude dripping from her tone.

LOW KEY FALLIN' FOR A SAVAGE 3

"It's me, I came to pick up Yo'Sahn," I spat back with the same energy as her. She really had no reason to be so nasty when she'd gotten paid for her services, and since Yoshi was old enough to keep himself entertained, then she'd really gotten paid for nothing.

"I sent him with his damn daddy! Y'all took too long comin back!"

"You did *what*!" I was hoping that I'd heard her wrong because there wasn't no way that my own mama would give my child to his no-good ass daddy. It wasn't like she wasn't aware of his triflin ways, so that meant that she *knowingly* gave my baby to that nigga.

"I *said* I sent him with his daddy, Destiny. I told yo sister that I had some shit to do! Y'all shouldn't have took so damn long!" she had the nerve to say like that gave her an excuse. I was fuming and instantly started dialing up Antonio's stupid ass.

"You know damn well he don't be havin my son! You got me fucked-up Adina! On my soul, I'm gone beat yo ass if anything happens to him!" I gritted as the phone rang in my ear until the voicemail picked up, and I called his ass right back.

Without giving her a chance to reply, I stormed out to my car, still waiting for him to pick up the phone. At this point, he'd basically kidnapped my baby, and I was mad as hell. Not only had Yo'Sahn not seen him consistently in years, but he knew damn well he didn't have the right to just come and get him. I was so mad at my mama it took everything in me not to try and drag her drunk ass out of her building. After receiving the voicemail for the third time, I decided to leave him a message as I got in my car.

"Tone, you a bitch nigga, on my soul! You don't want to play with me right now, I swear to God if I don't get my son back *tonight*, I'm gone fuck you up!" I couldn't believe the nerve of that nigga to think that any of the shit he was doing was okay.

He'd already gotten me in DCFS crosshairs with his first

13

stunt and now, he was snatching my kid up like he had any rights to him. Frustrated tears fell from my eyes, and I quickly wiped them away, even more upset that I was crying, but after the day I'd had, I couldn't stop myself. Eazy was laid up in the hospital, Trell was dead, and now my baby was with a nigga he didn't know from a can of paint! As emotional as I was, I started up my car and pulled off headed towards the last apartment that I knew of Antonio staying at. While I drove, I went to his mama's contact, glad that I'd saved it despite not having used it in, I don't know how long. She, just like her son, was very active in Yo'Sahn's life at one point, but slowly tapered off in time. It bothered me at first how easy it was for her to forget about my son, but after a while, I became too busy to even care. I gave my all to raising him the best way that I could, and I figured that it was their loss if they didn't want to be a part of his life. Now when I'd found Juice and Yo'Sahn seemed to be doing better, they wanted to try and creep their way back into the picture, and I wasn't having that.

Thankfully, she answered right away like she'd been sitting by the phone. "Hello? Antonio?"

"No, ma'am, it's Destiny. I was wondering if Antonio had been there with Yo'Sahn today?" I held my breath, waiting for her to reply.

"Hell, yeah! He's here now. Antonio left bout an hour and a half ago talking about going to get him some food, and I ain't heard from his ass since!" she fussed irritably, and I sighed in relief. It was just like him to pick Yo'Sahn up, only to drop him the fuck off with somebody else, and he wondered why they couldn't build a good relationship.

"I'm on my way right now. I'll be there in fifteen minutes," I said in a rush.

She was still talking when I hung up the phone and sped towards her house that was actually closer to where I was on Halsted. I was damn near running lights to get to Yo'Sahn, and I made it in less than ten minutes. As soon as I pulled up, Antonio's Cutlass was swerving into the space behind me, damn near hitting the back of my shit because he barely put it in park before jumping out.

"Nigga, you got some nerve taking my fuckin baby!" I'd abandoned my trek to the door to turn around and meet him on the sidewalk, swinging as soon as I was within arm's reach. He struggled to get ahold of my arms as I swung wildly, trying to land a punch anywhere that I could.

"Destiny, Destiny, calm the fuck down!"

"Fuck you!" I gritted, fighting to get out of his hold. By now, he had me in a bear hug with my back to his front as I bucked. Growing increasingly more enraged, I threw my head back catching him in the face, and he instantly released me with a groan.

"Ahh, you crazy ass bitch!"

I turned around to see him holding his nose with both hands as blood slipped between his fingers. He'd stumbled back a few feet away from me and the same bitch from the hospital appeared out of nowhere, trying to console him. She must have been in the car with him the whole time and had only just now decided to step out but ask me if I gave a fuck. If she was smart, she'd leave me alone or she'd be bleeding right next to her nigga.

"You ain't seen crazy! Stay the fuck away from my son!" I hit them both with a warning look before continuing to the porch where his mama and Yo'Sahn stood, watching in horror. Mrs. Green was already crying and fussing as he stepped down to where I was. I ignored every slur she was saying and walked back to my car, passing Antonio on the way. He was lucky all he'd gotten was a possibly broken nose because next time, I was going to shoot his black ass.

An hour later, I'd fed Yo'Sahn, and he was in his room doing homework. He'd been mad as hell that his many calls to Juice and Eazy had gone unanswered, and I had to break down and tell him what happened. As strong as he was, finding out about Eazy had him damn near in tears, even though I'd let him know that he was doing okay. They'd barely gotten better after getting shot themselves and another man that he looked up to had almost died. I didn't know what to say to him to lift his spirits, so when he asked to be excused, I'd allowed him to go ahead to his room while I cleaned up our dishes.

Now, I was trying to relax in the tub and wash away the stress from today's events, but it was definitely not working. It didn't help that I still had yet to talk to Juice, and I was worried about his ugly ass. I knew that he was feeling some type of way about his brother and Trell, but he needed to understand that if we were together, he'd have to communicate better. Disappearing for hours after hearing such bad news was not going to fly with me. For all I knew, he could have been somewhere dead or in jail for killing some damn body.

Shaking my head at how quickly that thought had worsened my mood, I decided to get out of the bath. It wasn't working to calm my nerves anyway, and I figured I should probably call the police stations and hospitals just in case. Juice was a hothead, so it wasn't far-fetched for him to have gone out and done something crazy to get himself locked up. I'd definitely rather him be in jail than dead or hurt in any way. Wrapping one of his plush black towels around my body, I carefully stepped out of the tub since his ass didn't have a rug on the floor and made my way back into the bedroom. Imagine my surprise, when I saw Juice laid out across the bed on his back with an arm thrown across his eyes. My emotional ass was instantly ready to cry from a mixture of happiness and sadness. I was happy that he was home in one piece, but I was sad for him. He'd lost a friend and almost lost his brother in the same day, so I knew he was feeling fucked-up, but he'd never admit it. Without saying anything, I climbed on top of him and laid down on his bare chest since he'd stripped down to his boxers.

"I know this is a stupid question, but are you okay?" I asked quietly as he wrapped his arms around me. After everything, just being this close to him had me feeling secure, and I snuggled deeper into his embrace.

He sighed deeply and ran his fingers across my shoulders. "Nah, you straight. I can't lie though; I'm pissed the fuck off. I'm ready to burn this muhfucka down, to find Budda, but I needed to come and make sure y'all was straight first. This shit is new to me, so I gotta remember that you, Yo'Sahn, and this baby need me too," he paused, and I felt him adjust slightly so he could look down at me.

Damn if my insides didn't melt from his admission. It was rare, but there were times when Juice had the ability to make me swoon. Something about having a nigga that was so rough around the edges, show that he gave a fuck was enough to have me weak in the knees like SWV. I thought about telling him what had happened with Antonio but thought better of it. He already had a ton of shit on his plate, and I didn't want to add my baby daddy drama to the mix, at least not yet anyway.

"I'm sorry about ....*everything*." I sat up so that I could meet his gaze, feeling bad about the sadness there. I was used to him being strong and completely confident but looking at him now, I could see how unsure he was.

"As long as you're good, then we are too," I simpered, meaning every word. Just having him back safe and sound had given me a sense of calm and my worries had vanished but knowing Juice the way I did I knew that would be short-lived.

BUDDA

"Sit yo ass down, Olivia!" I barked, narrowing my eyes at her as she jumped and snapped the curtain closed. She'd been checking the window ever since we'd checked into the hotel and at this point, I was ready to wring her fucking neck. Her paranoia was putting me on edge and was quickly making me regret bringing her along. What the fuck did I need with a scary ass bitch? Truthfully, she was probably jonesing, and I'd neglected to get us any coke before leaving, so she was struck for now. The only thing that was keeping me calm at the moment was piles of cash that laid scattered across the bed. Seeing that much money after all these years had my dick hard as fuck and knowing that it came from Eazy, made the lick that much sweeter. He should have known better than to ever cross ME! I was the one that looked out for him when every other hustler had turned their backs. I was the one who gave him advice when he felt like he couldn't go to his old man. It was ME! And the nigga had the nerve to basically spit in my face. Not only did he fail to look out, but he fucked around and stole my bitch. There was no way I could let that slide and stealing his money and killing Trell was just the beginning.

"I can't help it, Budda! What if somebody saw us? What if they find my car?" Olivia was already talking that nonsense that was going to make me fuck her up. I shot her a look that had her plopping down on the bed in a huff with her arms crossed.

"Nobody saw shit, if they did, we would've been booked already! Now, shut yo dumb ass up, better yet, take a fucking nap!" I eyed her until she finally laid down, facing me like that would make me feel bad for her or some shit.

"I don't wanna take a nap, Budda! I need a hit baaaad I won't be able to sleep without it!" Despite the whining she was doing, she knew not to sit up. I had to stop myself from laughing at how ridiculous she looked laying there and saying that she didn't wanna take a nap. Being honest, I needed a little something myself, even though I was already on a high just from our activities that day.

"I'll go in a minute! Take yo dumb ass to sleep!" I spat absent-mindedly and put my focus back on the TV since she'd distracted me long enough.

There hadn't been any news coverage of the shootout at the club yet or about what happened to Trell, and I was waiting to see what damage had been done. With any luck, Dre was able to catch that nigga, Eazy, off guard and die in the process. There was no way I was going to share my earnings with him, so on the slight chance that he got away, I was going to be the one to put a bullet in his head. Cousin or not, there was only room for one nigga at the top. My ears perked up as soon as I saw the outside of the club flash across the screen, and I cut the volume up as high as it would go. They weren't releasing the names of any of the people that had died, but the minute that they said the club's owner was rushed to the hospital, I wanted to spit fire! That only meant that the nigga was showing signs of life, and I'd been hoping for him to be dead on arrival.

"Arrrgggh!" Jumping up off my chair, I went to knock the cheap ass lamp off the side table and instantly grit my teeth as

19

pain shot up my arm. Cheap ass motel had the shit bolted down, and all I'd managed to do was hurt my damn self.

"What! What's wrong, Budda!" Olivia was sitting up, looking wide-eyed at my outburst. I ignored her as I paced the floor and prayed that the nigga died in the ambulance. I needed to get out of there! If there was any chance that Eazy survived, it would put a huge dent in my plans. I didn't even know how serious his injuries were, so the nigga could possibly be getting stitched up and released at this very moment. After this shit and Trell being dead, they would definitely be on high alert which could be a big problem for me, and now I didn't even have Dre's bitch ass to fall back on. I grabbed up a couple of bills off the bed and hit Olivia with a death stare.

"Stay yo dumb ass here, and don't touch shit!" I growled, stuffing the money down into my pocket and left the room without giving her a chance to speak. There was a lot of shit on my mind, and I couldn't think straight while sitting in that cramped ass room. The minute I got outside; I noticed the scratches on the car from when I side-swiped Trell.

My adrenaline was still pumping when we'd first arrived, so I hadn't paid it any attention, but now my anxiousness was through the roof, and the shit was looking way more obvious even without the sun shining bright. Cursing under my breath as I inspected the damage, I made a mental note to stop by a junk yard tomorrow, so that I could get rid of it before sliding into the driver's seat. My main focus at the moment was to get high and try to come up with another plan that would land me on top.

EAZY

I woke up to Dream pacing around the room as she spoke on the phone in a hushed voice, but the second she saw my eyes opened, she immediately hung up and was at my bedside.

"Oh, thank God you're up!" she gasped, wiping away the tears that covered her face. I was still trying to work through what was going on as she rambled and pressed the button for the nurse. A vague image of a showdown with Dre's bitch ass flashed through my mind, reminding me of why I was in the hospital in the first place, and my jaw clenched in anger. That nigga had come through my place of business like rambo, with his villain speech in tow. At first, I tried to stall him so that I could reach my gun, but when he mentioned my mother, all bets were off. To have him in my face bragging about what he'd done to her was some shit I still couldn't get off my mind. The only consolation that I had was being able to kill his ass, and I was grateful that I hadn't gone out with him, but there was still the matter of Budda. Before I could fix my mouth to ask Dream anything, the doctor came flying into the room with a nurse right behind her.

"Hello, Elijah. I'm Dr. White, and this is your nurse, Evelyn. She's going to take your vitals while I briefly go over everything with you," she explained while the nurse came around and took Dream's position on the side of me.

"Aight." I gave a quick nod, looking between her and Evelyn as she placed a small cuff around my wrist.

"Well, you were brought in yesterday with six gunshot wounds. We managed to remove each of the bullets, and you were also given a transfusion due to all of the blood loss. You're set to make a full recovery, and I'll be sure to monitor your progress over the next two weeks—"

"Hold up, I can't stay in here for no two weeks!" I cut in, shaking my head emphatically. I'd been following everything she said, but there was no way I was going to be staying in a hospital bed for that long. Dr. White looked alarmed by my outburst and immediately, looked to Dream like that was going to change my mind.

"Elijah—"

"Dream, I'm going home," I interrupted whatever it was she was about to say, setting my stern eyes on her. She looked like she hadn't gotten any sleep and stress covered her face. While I appreciated her presence considering what we had going on, I still wasn't going to commit to remaining in the hospital. Especially, when her ex was running around wreaking havoc on my family. Seeing that I wasn't about to argue over the shit, she clamped her mouth shut with a huff and folded her arms over her chest.

"Okay, well, you always have the option to discharge, but I strongly advise against it. I would implore you to stay the entire two weeks, so that we can monitor your progress and you can allow your body to rest," she paused to look over the vitals that the nurse handed to her, "Your vitals are getting stronger, which is a good thing, but I'll leave you two to talk this over. In the meantime, would you like something for pain?"

As bad as I wanted to refuse since I was pissed off, I couldn't deny the nagging pain that was radiating all over my body. "Yeah, I'd appreciate it," I gritted, sending her on her way while Dream mugged me irritably. She waited until they had left the room before she started going in on me.

"You not leavin this hospital, Elijah." The authority in her tone had me chuckling, which only made her frown deepen. "You think this is a joke? You were just shot almost as many times as 50 Cent and instead of staying here like the doctor told you, you're trying to discharge early? What do you even think you're going to be able to do in this state anyway?" She called herself going off, but little did she know, she looked and sounded comical as hell especially bringing up 50 Cent.

"Yo you trippin, right now. Where the fuck Juice and my pops at while they left yo little ass here to try and boss me around?" I questioned, instantly making her demeanor change. She went right from aggressive to her shoulders slumping, putting me on high alert.

"Elijah, I…." her voice trailed off, and she looked away as the nurse returned with my meds. I peeped her breathe a sigh of relief, but if she thought I wasn't going to further question her ass about her odd behavior, then she had me fucked up. As soon as I swallowed the pills, I was brought and the nurse left, I looked her way with expectant eyes.

"Finish what you was sayin," I ordered, watching her closely.

"I figured that Juice would want to be the one to tell you, but….Trell was shot yesterday too… he didn't make it."

I swear, it felt like somebody punched me in my stomach after hearing some news like that. Falling back onto my pillows, I squeezed my eyes shut, hoping that I hadn't heard her right even though I knew, I had. Something as serious as Trell getting killed would be the only reason why my brother wouldn't be here for me. That nigga was like a brother to us, so I knew that Juice was taking the shit hard, especially after me being shot

23

too. I willed myself not to cry, but that shit didn't work, and a couple of tears managed to slip from my eyes. I quickly wiped them away, vowing that I was going to kill whoever had taken him out.

"Give me yo phone," I said, ignoring everything else that Dream was saying as she tried to comfort me. Sighing, she handed it to me, and I immediately called Juice.

"Yo, Dream. I'm gone be back up there in a sec, I got held up over here at the house," he explained as soon as the call connected.

"Nigga, it's me, I need you to bring me some clothes and shit up here. I'm leavin *tonight*." After learning about Trell, I knew I had to get out of there, so he wouldn't be left alone to handle whoever had done this shit.

"Aw damn, bro I'm glad you up, but I don't know bout you tryna leave and shit—"

"I already know about Trell," I gritted, locking eyes with Dream briefly. "I'm getting the fuck outta here, regardless, but it'd be easier if you helped me."

"Fuck man, I'll be there in a minute," he cursed and hung up, clearly pissed off, but I didn't give a fuck.

I tossed Dream her phone back, satisfied that I'd gotten something taken care of, but looking at the saddened expression on her face, I knew there was some more shit that I needed to handle. We'd been fucked-up for a minute and despite all of the shit that I'd done, she'd been there for me every time I'd needed her. I still had yet to officially apologize to her for jumping to conclusions and messing up what we had going on. I'd fucked up a good thing and wasted precious time that I wouldn't be able to get back. Hopefully, it wasn't too late to fix things though. She was already getting prepared to leave when I called her name to stop her.

"Dream, what you leavin for?"

Slinging her purse over her shoulder, she met my eyes with

her tear-filled ones. "I'm going home. You're alright enough to leave, and Juice is on his way back sooo..." she allowed her voice to trail off.

"What him comin got to do with shit? I need you here just like I need him... maybe even more." I meant exactly what I was saying, and I hoped that she could see that. If I didn't understand how much I needed her before, I damn sure did now. Ever since I'd fucked Dream over, things had been going downhill, and it felt like I was spiraling out of control. Despite it all, she'd still been showing me love, and I was starting to realize that *this* was the shit I'd been looking for all this time. The type of love that was there even in the midst of pain. Dream had been giving me that and more, but I'd been too blind and too damn stupid to see.

"I-I can't do this with you right now, Elijah."

"Then when, huh! You been runnin from me long enough! I know I'm fucked up—no I ain't *shit* for the way I been acting, and I'd rip my heart out my chest right now and give it to you just to make it right. I'm tryna do the next best thing though. A nigga trying to apologize *and* give you my heart in more than just the physical sense."

I felt like I was pleading for my life right now and in a way, I was. A mixture of doubt and fear clouded her eyes, but I wasn't about to take no for an answer. She went to speak, and I cut her off. "Tell me you don't still love me! Say you don't want me to fight for you!"

A spark lit up in her face, and she raised a brow in question. "Will you leave me alone if I do?" I didn't even need a minute to think on it before I shook my head no.

"I'd be lying if I said I would, so I won't even put that shit in yo head." I shrugged, not caring how she took my answer. It was the truth, whether or not she wanted to lie about her feelings, I still wasn't going to let her walk away from me. Besides, actions speak louder than words, and her actions told me that she loved me. I'd bet money on that!

She laughed bitterly, planting a hand on her wide hips. "See, that's where you got me fucked up at! Just because *you* finally decided to get your head out of your ass, doesn't mean I have to be receptive! I've given you plenty of chances to get your shit together, nigga, and you shitted on me *every* time. But now since you've had a come to Jesus moment, I'm supposed to fall at your feet? I won't deny that I love you, Elijah, but just because you love somebody it doesn't mean they're good for you, and *you* are the very *worst* thing for me." Just that quick, she'd read me my rights and slipped out of the room, leaving me dumbfounded. I mean, sure I knew it would take more than a desperate ass plea, but I wasn't expecting for her to check my ass and leave. Regardless of her rejection, she'd still unintentionally told me that she still loved me, and that was all I needed to continue my pursuit.

DREAM

I left the hospital mad as hell, and I didn't know why. Matter of fact, I knew exactly why! Elijah King Jr.! He had the biggest set of balls I'd ever seen on a nigga to try and use that moment to seek my forgiveness. I saw right through his shit, and it was obvious that he was trying to use his condition for a sympathy reconciliation. When I damn near begged the raggedy muthafucka, he gave me his ass to kiss, and now he wanted me to allow him back into my life! Hell nah! I'd finally gained some piece of understanding about our relationship ending, and it'd taken a whole lot of SZA, Jhene Aiko, and Summer Walker, but it had been done... at least, I hoped so. A part of me was pulling back to him, and I had to fight that shit like the evil it was. I couldn't fall back victim to him. If being with him and Budda had taught me anything, it was that you can't keep letting shit slide. Every time that I forgave a nigga, it just told them that I was weak-willed, and that they had control of me, but I wasn't going to continue to make the same mistakes. I was too damn old to keep doing the same shit over and over again thinking that my loyalty would be matched.

Nope! I was done with love and everything that bitch had to offer.

"So, you just left?" Destiny gasped, clutching her chest with wide eyes.

"Hell, yeah! I got too much shit going on right now to deal with Elijah's confused ass!" I told her, smacking my lips irritably. I didn't miss the look of doubt she shot me, but thankfully, she didn't call me out. She did, however, try and plead a case for that nigga.

"Welllll, maybe he really means it," she dragged lowly, surprising the shit out of me. As far as I knew, Destiny was on my side when it came to Elijah, but now she was taking up for him.

I narrowed my eyes at her, and she held her hands up in surrender. "Hear me out, hoe. I ain't saying that he's off the hook, but I do think he realizes he fucked-up. You been moping around here all this time and still making yourself available to his ass when he needs you. Maybe getting shot done knocked some sense into him, and now, he can see that you didn't deserve that shit. I don't think you should jump right back into anything with him, but at least let the nigga grovel a lil bit." She shrugged, making me frown. I'd come over after I left the hospital, so that I could vent and we could talk shit about his ass together, and here she was doing the exact opposite. Call me petty, but I wasn't trying to hear this "give him a chance" shit she was talking. I couldn't deny that me trying to be there for him time and time again had probably given away that I still loved his dirty draws, but that didn't mean that I wanted anything to do with him.

"Naw, he can keep that apology and shove it up Sherice's pregnant ass."

"Girl, boom! You know that bitch was probably lying through them cheap ass veneers," Destiny waved me off with a roll of her eyes, "that's all desperate hoes know how to do is lie."

"Well, she wouldn't be able to lie about it if he hadn't fucked her in the first place with his paranoid ass." I gave her a pointed look, and before she could come back with a rebuttal, Yoshi came into the room.

"Ma, can I ride with Juice to go see Eazy?" He leaned against the doorframe with hopeful eyes. I could see that his mama was hesitant about letting him leave with Juice or just letting him go in general after the shit that Antonio had pulled.

"Dang, Destiny, I ain't know I was invisible," I teased since he didn't speak.

"My bad, wassup, TeTe?" he spoke and then turned back to his mama. "So, can I?" Even though I knew that Destiny was only being cautious, I still tapped her on the leg and nodded for her to go ahead and let him go.

Once Elijah left the hospital, he was going to be in full-blown revenge mode, which would leave even less time for Yoshi than he'd already been getting. She smacked her lips but nodded that he could go, prompting him to run off excitedly before she could change her mind. A second later, Juice filled the doorway looking just like his ugly ass brother, but that didn't stop the glow from filling Destiny's face upon seeing him, even though she tried to hide it behind rolling her eyes.

"What's good, Dream?" He sent a head nod my way, and I forced myself to give him a weak flick of my wrist, followed by a grimace that he must've mistaken for a smile because he focused back on Destiny and dropped a quick kiss on her lips. "Bae, you said that lil nigga could ride with me?"

If I wasn't in such a shitty mood, I'd probably be able to admit how cute they were, but I was so I was in a shitty mood, so I focused on the huge flat screen that Juice had hanging on the wall.

"Yeah, and you better make sure he comes back to me the same way I sent him, or I'm gone fuck you and Eazy up!" she snapped, narrowing her eyes up at him. A confident grin came over his face at the idle threat, and he went to kiss her again.

"I got him, I promise." This time, when he spoke, it was much lower to let her know that he was serious. The two made eye contact for a second before that playful grin came back, and he rubbed her small pudge. "You just make sure you be good and feed my lil princess in there."

"Stop sayin that!"

He laughed, moving out of the way, barely dodging the fist she swung at him. "Why, it's still gone be a girl. Don't be takin yo frustrations out on her while I'm gone either, she'll tell me if you do." Despite the scowl on her face, Destiny was clearly enamored by everything that had to do with Juice. She mocked him with exaggerated facial expressions but allowed him another kiss.

"His ass stay callin my baby a damn girl," she fussed the second he left the room, after promising to return shortly.

"Only y'all silly muthafuckas would be arguing about what the baby is." My shoulders shook as I laughed at them. I hadn't even been there a whole thirty minutes, and their bickering had taken my mind off of Elijah's mess. "What Yo'Sahn want it to be?" I asked since he hadn't too much mentioned the baby since finding out that his mama was pregnant.

"Surprisingly, he on Juice's team girl train." Her tone was an indication of how unhappy she was by that, and I couldn't deny that I was shocked myself. I would've thought that he'd want another boy around.

"Well, if it makes you feel any better, I don't care what the sex is as long as TeTe's baby comes out healthy and fat," I said, reaching over and rubbing her belly, only for her to slap my hand away.

"Well, it don't! If I have a girl, I swear Juice gone be raising her lil ass by himself. You, him, and Yo'Sahn."

"Biiiitch, I don't know how Juice be puttin up with all that damn attitude." I laughed, knowing that he was catching hell behind this baby, and that it would probably only get worse after it came out a girl, like he predicted. I didn't want to make her anymore pissed than she already was, but the chances of her having a girl were beginning to look more and more likely. With the way she was acting, I wanted her to have one just so I could see how she'd react, even though I knew no matter how mad she got, she'd still be the best mother ever. Definitely better than our raggedy ass mama.

"He don't put up with shit with his ugly ass. He's barely here between trying to run things and find Budda." The mention of my ex instantly had my shoulders tensing. I hadn't gotten anything else from him in a while, but that was obviously because his crazy ass had been out here trying to start a war.

"I can't wait til they finally do find his bitch ass," I grumbled just as a text came through from Ashley, asking about my progress with the shop. She wasn't the only one that had hit me up worried about their jobs, but I had yet to answer any of their calls or texts. I couldn't face them, knowing that I had basically failed them, especially since I still wasn't having any luck getting a loan. Not even bothering to open it, I set my phone to the side and focused back on the conversation that me and Destiny were having.

* * *

I STAYED WITH MY SISTER UNTIL JUICE CAME BACK A COUPLE OF hours later. Just like he'd promised, Yo'Sahn was perfectly fine and in a really good mood after finally being able to see Elijah. I would've stayed longer but seeing them all over each other only made me miss Eazy's no good ass more, despite how bad I wanted to slap him. It was all for the better though because I had a brand new bottle of wine that I could drown my sorrows in, and I planned to do that as soon as I got home.

31

I pulled up at home with a nice bath and a glass of wine on my mind, so when I saw five niggas running between my crib and a van carrying shit, I was ready to go off. Without thinking, I stormed right up to the first one I saw making his way back out to the van.

"What the fuck you think you doin!" I snapped, spraying him with mace before he could answer. His hands instantly went to his eyes as he yelled out, drawing his crew back outside.

"Yooo, what the fuck you just spray me for!" At this point, he was damn near clawing out his eyes as his friends came over to try and help, but a wave of my arm had them backing away quickly.

"Aye, Dream chill, man. We here for Eazy!" one of them called.

"Eazy?" My brows snapped together in confusion at the mention of Elijah and from this nigga knowing my name.

"Yeah, he inside," he added, trying to watch me and his friend, who was still doubled over and moaning in pain. Honestly, I had probably used the entire can on his ass and didn't even have anymore, but that didn't stop me from threatening the others with it. "He just got us dropping off some shit for him. I swear, go check, he in there with his nurse."

Still unsure, I eased closer so that I could see for myself, prompting them all to move out of my way since I was still holding up my mace defensively. I didn't trust shit, especially since Eazy had just gotten shot up the day before. For all I knew, these niggas were coming to hurt me in an effort to get to him, and I wasn't taking any chances. I stepped inside of my house cautiously and made sure to close and lock the door behind me just in case my suspicions were correct. My living room had different medical supplies stacked in a corner, and I could vaguely hear conversation in the back. With at least part of dude's story confirmed, I finally dropped my arm and stomped all the way to my bedroom where Elijah sat lounging with his back against the head board and his feet kicked up. A nurse fluttered about the room giving him orders, but she quieted once she saw me looming in the doorway.

"Oh shit, welcome home, baby." He cheesed widely. "Aye, Deb, this my girl, Dream. Dream, meet Deb."

"Nigga, is you out your mind?" I spat, ignoring his introduction and leaving Ms. Deb dumbfounded. My eye was starting to twitch fucking around with Elijah. I mean like, who would do some shit like this besides one of the fucking King brothers?

"What you mean, I told you I needed you, right?" His face showed genuine concern at my reaction like he really thought I wanted him to chase me down or some shit. Already, I was getting a damn headache. I really wanted to kick him, his nurse, and his group of movers out of my shit, and I should have. No matter how much I didn't want to be around him, I did want him to get better and moving around with fresh wounds probably wouldn't do him any good. *Damn that fucking Juice for not saying shit.* I couldn't wait to see him again, I was going to fuck him up since I couldn't do shit to his brother.

JUICE

*J*t had been a couple of days since Eazy had taken it upon himself to leave the hospital, and I was still surprised that I'd only gotten one call from Dream, so far. The day I dropped his crazy ass off at her crib, she called and cussed me the fuck out. She even had her sister trying to jump on the band wagon and add her two cents, which didn't mean shit to me. All it took was some dick to make her take her pregnant ass to sleep and leave me alone, but even if she didn't want to admit it, she wanted Dream and Eazy to get their shit together just as much as I did. I was glad he'd finally saw his wrongdoings in the situation and was trying to right them, because I didn't know how much more of his sour ass attitude I could take. These days, I was chain smoking blunts just to deal with him and Destiny's worrisome asses. Like now, I'd just finished smoking before leaving the crib because I already knew that today's events would be stress-inducing.

I pulled up to Dream's crib and got out just as Eazy's nurse made her way down the sidewalk. As we passed each other, I admired the way her thick body filled the uniform she wore perfectly. Like any other female that knew she'd caught my eye, shorty put an extra sway in her hips and slowed down.

"Heyyy, Juice," she greeted me and bit into her bottom lip seductively.

"Sup Deb." I kept it short and went to keep it moving. Looking was one thing, but I wasn't beat for conversation with her ass. She, on the other hand, had something else in mind.

"Damn, I can't get a second of your time?" Stopping in the middle of the sidewalk, she planted a hand on her hip and looked me up and down with lust in her eyes. I didn't even try to hide the chuckle in my voice as I fully turned her way. This wasn't the first time I'd been tested, and she damn sure wasn't the finest bitch that had come at me, but I wasn't even about to play with my girl like that. She must have taken my laughter as me entertaining her flirting because her smile widened with confidence.

"I ain't even gone play you, shorty, the problems my girl gone bring you from fucking with me ain't the kind you want. Her crazy ass probably watching right now, ready to jump out the bushes and beat yo ass," I warned, adding to her fear by looking around, like Destiny could really be out there hiding and shit. It was hilarious the way her face cracked, before she took off in the other direction without another word.

I entered the front door and ran straight into Dream, who was wearing a deep scowl. "You came to get yo aggravating ass brother?" she questioned, looking like she was on her way out.

"Quit acting like you don't want that nigga here," I teased, grinning down at her as she rolled her eyes. She could pretend all she wanted, but I knew she wanted him there, and that's why she hadn't tried to complain to me since that first day.

"Tuh," she sucked her teeth and continued on her way out the door.

Unfazed, I went in search of my brother, finding him in the bedroom already dressed in a white tee and some black sweats.

"What's good, bro." We slapped hands and he had me help him into his wheelchair.

"Nigga, what you over here doin to my future sister-in-law?" I asked, following behind him as he wheeled himself into the living room. I moved a few of the pillows she had on the couch and plopped down to await his answer.

"I ain't did shit to her. She just in a funky mood cause of Deb's thot ass. I'm callin the agency tomorrow, so they can send somebody else out here cause the bitch tryna ruin my relationship."

"But you ain't in a relationship though." From the evil expression he shot my way, I knew he wasn't happy about me pointing out his one-sided relationship. It wasn't my fault his ass forced his way in her crib, and she wasn't happy about it. Little did he know, he was in for more bad news once Pierre arrived.

"Man, fuck you!" he quipped just as knocking sounded at the door. "Go get the door with yo shit talkin ass."

He was aware that our connect was stopping through, but he had no idea what Pierre was coming for. Since Pops didn't want his ass around, regardless of him actually saving Eazy, he'd demanded that he stay away from him. Me, on the other hand, I appreciated him stepping up despite his past actions and helping my boy out. It was crazy how mature I was thinking these days; who would've thought that a baby would have me out here on some grown man shit? With a weak shrug, I went and let Pierre in. I shook his hand before showing him to the living room where Eazy was waiting. Of course, his bodyguards were right behind him, looking uncomfortable as hell in their tight ass suits.

"Get y'all big sumo wrestler-lookin asses on in here too and try not to break shit in this lil ass apartment." I moved out of the way to give them more room in the cramped hallway, and they filled the entire space, hitting me with ice grills as they shuffled through, following Pierre. After locking the door, I made my way back into the living room, sitting down in the chair closest to Eazy and across from Pierre and his goons.

"First, let me just say that I'm sorry about Trell, I understand that he was a big part of y'all organization, and a close family friend. If you'd let me, I'd like to cover his funeral costs, just to take a little bit off your plates," he said, looking between the two of us.

I personally wasn't opposed to him stepping in and helping us out with that, considering that we had so much other shit to handle, but Eazy was already shaking his head no.

"I appreciate it, but we've already got it taken care of." His answer had my brows knitting together in confusion. The nigga had just got his ass out the hospital, and we hadn't talked about shit regarding Trell's funeral, but I wouldn't call him out on it.

"I figured you did," Pierre gave a short nod and continued, "anyway, it's good to see you alive and well—"

"Look, you ain't gotta hit me with all these pleasantries. I know you here about your money, and we already on top of it. This shit ain't nothing but a minor setback." Eazy motioned to the wheelchair and his injuries, prompting Pierre's brows to dip slightly before he glanced my way. The surprise on his face told me that he expected Eazy to already know what he was really in town for, and it didn't have shit to do with his money. We'd been working with Pierre for years, so he knew we were thorough, and that little bit of money that Budda had gotten away with could easily be taken care of.

"That money is the least of my concerns, Elijah, I'm actually not here on business... I came because you were shot, and as your father, I had to make sure you were straight."

Silence fell over the room as Eazy looked into each of our faces in disbelief. "Wait, nigga, what?" He stood up abruptly with a grimace on his face. Instinctively, Pierre's goons reached for their weapons at the sudden movement and off top, I stood too and drew my gun.

Seeing that things were about to get ugly, Pierre waved for them to back down, and they eased their hands away from their sides, still eyeing us. "You're my son, Eazy. Look, I know this shit sounds crazy, but me and Rachel were together. She was supposed to be my wife. I loved yo mama but unfortunately, with the money and notoriety came a bunch hoes and niggas looking to take my spot. She ended up leaving me and getting with EK, but she was already pregnant with you. I didn't even find out shit about you until you were about three. The day I saw you though, I knew you were mine, and I didn't need to ask any questions or shit! Me and Rachel got into right there, and I snatched yo lil ass up! Not only had she left me, but she named you after that nigga and wasn't even gone tell me!" he gritted, looking pissed off like that shit had just happened today and not over twenty-five years ago. "I ain't even get you off the block before some bitch ass nigga shot my car up, and I realized what she had been saying about how dangerous this shit was. Way too dangerous to be trying to raise a toddler around, so we made an agreement that her and EK would take care of you and I'd stay away. The only problem was that this shit was in your blood, so you ended up finding me anyway. I figured the least I could do was look out for you and make sure you were good out here, and you been cool so far. Shit, better than I could have expected, honestly."

"Can you fuckin believe this shit!" Eazy shook his head, turning to me with his forehead bunched.

"Shiiiit, I mean at first I didn't, not even when Pops told me, but the nigga gave you blood for your transfusion. If ain't nothin else true, you definitely his son," I told him, releasing a heavy sigh. The confusion written on my brother's face made me feel bad for him. It wasn't enough that he'd been shot the fuck up, but our best friend and mama had been killed, we'd been robbed by his fuckin mentor, and now he was finding out that our connect was his pops. If it was me, I'd be ready to shoot some shit up starting with this little ass apartment, but of course, Eazy wasn't on that shit.

"Son, I'm not trying to come here and start no issues, but I did think it was time you knew the truth. I really do want to have a relationship with you, but it's no pressure. You got the number." Pierre stood up from his seat and nodded in my direction before seeing himself out. As soon as the door closed behind him, Eazy looked at me like he was ready to take my head off.

"Don't look at me like that, that shit between you, Pops, and that nigga," I huffed, putting my gun away. "You need to sit yo ass down before I have to drive yo cripple ass back to the hospital."

"Nigga, fuck you," he sneered but took a seat like I told him to.

"That shit crazy though, right? They old asses had some love triangle shit going on."

"Man, I ain't even bouta worry bout that shit, right now. I'll deal with his ass after we take care of Budda."

He winced as he tried to make himself comfortable. It didn't take a rocket scientist to figure out that he was trying to avoid the situation. He'd probably still be going out of his way not to address it even after we caught up with Budda, but that was his business. As long as he knew, then it was his decision whether or not he wanted to try and have a father-son relationship with Pierre.

DESTINY

"*O*h, I know this nigga didn't!" I held the paper up to my nose as if that would help me see better, but there was no mistaking the official document.

Antonio had really gone through with his threats and was summoning me to court for custody of Yo'Sahn. Even though I knew there was no way in hell a judge would give his unfit ass custody of a turtle let alone my son, it still enraged me to know that he'd even go so far. I tried to control the features in my face so that Juice and Yoshi, who were still sitting in the car, wouldn't see that something was wrong. We were on our way to my second appointment, which would also be my big gender reveal, and I was already in a mood at the possibility that Juice was right about it being a girl. I was so nervous that I'd had him stop by my apartment, so I could check the mail in an attempt to stall, and now, I had even more of a reason to be irritated. Blowing out an aggravated breath, I stuffed the paper down into my purse along with my other mail and made my way back to the car.

"You good, now, or do you want to stop and get the car washed too?" Juice teased as soon as I slammed the door shut behind me, making Yoshi burst into a fit of chuckles. I shot them both a murderous glare that only made them laugh harder. "Calm that attitude down. It ain't no point in stallin, bae. We might as well just gone head and find out lil baby, a girl. I'll even take yo greedy ass out for crab legs after since I'm such a good sport and shit." With his fingers intertwined with mine, he lifted my hand and kissed it, grinning sexily.

At the mention of crab legs, my attitude with him melted away. Girl or boy, this baby loved food and definitely loved some crabs. I decided to put the custody thing into the back of my mind along with my ill feelings of having a girl. It seemed to make Juice happy and considering that he didn't have much to be happy about these days, it was the least I could do. Not only had they not found Budda, but they'd had to bury Trell a few weeks back and although he hadn't said anything, I knew it was weighing heavily on him. I couldn't fight the smile that broke through as he rubbed my belly and then put his hand back in mine.

"See, I knew food would make my baby happy." Cheesing, he pulled off, not even flinching when I pinched his arm playfully. I couldn't flex, even though I couldn't stand his ass a majority of the time I *loved* what we had, and I loved even more the way that he showed Yo'Sahn how his mama should be treated. Despite our almost constant bickering, the way he cared for me was unmatched by anyone I'd ever been with, and Yoshi could see it too.

We pulled into the doctor's office and found a spot not too far from where Dream was parked. I'd invited my sister, so I wouldn't be outnumbered by team girl, but I was surprised to see Eazy step out of the car with her. From what she'd been telling me, she was still giving him a hard time despite his efforts, though I could see right through that shit. I might not have been too fond of him these days, but I had to admit that he was trying and was genuinely sorry about what he did to her. At least, he better had been.

"Heeeeey, big mama!" She walked up with a wide smile, instantly reaching in to rub my belly.

I rolled my eyes and resisted the urge to slap her hand away. "Big mama, my ass, I'm barely showing."

"Yeah, keep telling yourself that, preggers," Dream quickly dismissed, before turning to greet Yo'Sahn and Juice.

I was in denial about my growing stomach most days, but it was definitely getting bigger. With my face frowned up, I marched ahead of the group, a fresh attitude surfacing and just ready to get this shit over with. They were already getting on my nerves, and we hadn't even gotten in the building yet.

Everybody found a seat once we got inside except for Juice, who approached the desk to check-in, with me instantly drawing the eyes of every woman in the lobby, even the pregnant ones. I was beginning to get used to the attention that he got, but that didn't mean I was ever comfortable with it. Just like every other woman there, the nurse behind the desk was star struck looking up into his handsome face, and I quickly snapped my fingers, drawing her thirsty ass eyes my way. Of course, he thought that shit was funny, flashing all thirty-two of his perfect teeth, but he calmed all the way down seeing the look I gave him.

After giving her my name and appointment time, she let us know that a nurse would be with us shortly, and we went to sit and wait. It wasn't even five minutes later that my name was called, and we all made our way to the back. This time, the nurse was an older lady, which I appreciated because she knew how to keep her eyes to herself. She led us all into the small examination room where she checked my vitals and weight before leaving to go get the doctor.

"You ready to find out yo man been right this whole time?" Juice asked after helping me onto the table.

"Tuh, you swear you know everything, it could very well be a boy, and then what?"

Shrugging, he palmed my stomach. "Shiiiit I'm gone be cool either way, but I'm tellin you, this my lil girl. I'll make you a deal, though. As soon as Jerelisha is old enough, we can try for a boy."

"Jerelisha?"

"Jerelisha!" me and Dream questioned at the same time while Yo'Sahn and Eazy laughed.

"Boy, you crazy as hell if you think I'm naming my baby that shit!" I snickered, shaking my head, and this nigga really had the nerve to look surprised.

"What, you don't like it?"

"HELL NAW!" everybody, including Yoshi, shouted.

"Man, ain't nothing wrong with that name! Y'all on some hating ass shit!"

"Ain't nothing right with that muthafucka either. I might not want a girl, but I damn sure ain't gone name her *that*!" I snorted with an upturned nose. He had me fucked up if he thought there was a chance in hell, I'd name my baby that shit.

"We gone talk about this later," he grumbled lowly.

"Nah, bro, I don't think it's shit to talk about. I can't let you do my niece like that for real." Eazy could barely hide his laughter, but just as Juice went to speak, the doctor stepped in with wide eyes.

"Oh, we have an audience today, huh?" She smiled softly. "Hey, family. It's good to see you're taking good care of mommy, Jeremiah."

Juice ate up the compliment, unable to hide the pride on his face. "You already know, doc."

"Well, everything's looking good so far, but I take it you're all ready to find out what we're having," Dr. Reeves gushed. "You two still battling it out over the sex?" Her question was easily

43

answered by me groaning in Juice's annoying ass humming an "mmhmm."

"Well, hopefully, we can settle this debate once and for all, if baby decides to behave."

We all watched and quieted down as she prepared me for the ultrasound by squirting the warm jelly on my stomach and gearing up the machine. Almost instantly, the room was filled with the loud sounds of our baby's heartbeat. I had done this before with Yo'Sahn, but it was still just as exciting as if it was my first time being able to see my small love bug on the black and white screen.

"Okay, there's baby," Dr. Reeves pointed, showing us different body parts and making my anxiety shoot through the roof as I waited for her to reveal the sex. "Annnnnd, are you two ready?"

"No!"

"Hell, yeah!" Juice and I spoke at once.

"Uhhh, why don't y'all wait. That way I can throw y'all a gender reveal," Dream cut in, sensing my anxiousness.

I couldn't help but to let out a sigh of relief, since a gender reveal would buy me a couple more months to prepare myself. Juice, on the other hand, didn't look too pleased, however, he didn't put up the fight that I thought he would. With a stiff nod, he motioned for the doctor to go along with Dream's idea. I mouthed "thank you" and tooted up my lips, so he could plant a kiss on them while the doctor showed everyone else what the baby was on a sticky note. They all held a smirk on their faces, not alluding to whether or not it was a boy or girl, but I didn't even care. Honestly, I was just happy that the pressure was off.

"Alright, well I'll see you next month. Continue to keep your stress down and take your vitamins. It was nice to meet all of you," the doctor said before breezing right back out of the room. She'd barely been gone a second, and Juice was already trying to get them to tell him what the baby was. I should've known his ass wasn't going to be able to not know, thankfully, nobody even dropped a hint, which only had him more pressed.

He was still hounding them while I scheduled my next appointment, all the way up until we got out of the building. I could already tell that Yoshi and Eazy were going to be the weakest links, and he must have thought so too because he had them fall back, leaving me and Dream to ourselves.

"His ass think he slick, I hope they don't tell his black ass nothin," I huffed as we neared our cars. Since it was nearing the afternoon, the sun was beating down on me and the humidity had it almost too hot to breath.

It must have been fucking with Dream too because she was using the envelope with the baby's gender inside to fan herself. "Girl they ain't got shit to tell him. The doctor gave *me* the paper, Elijah just want to see him sweat." She giggled.

"How you pull that off?"

"Shiiiit, I just snatched the paper out of her hand before they got a good look. That nigga so thirsty to get on my good side that he didn't even try to put up a fight." Shrugging, she looked back at the guys with a small smile playing on her lips, and I knew exactly what that shit meant. She may have been putting up a good fight, but I could see she still wanted to be with Eazy.

"Sooo, you still playing hard to get or you letting him back in the honey pot?" Despite her dark complexion, Dream blushed, finally tearing her eyes away from them.

"Nah, he ain't off the hook yet, but I have been letting him try to wine and dine his way back in. I do feel kinda bad for him though, he still going through it from Trell's death, and he's trying hard not to deal with finding out Mr. King isn't actually his father."

Juice had told me all about Pierre being Eazy's daddy and that he wasn't taking it well. I could definitely understand where he was coming from after finding out some shit like that after all these years. I damn sure wouldn't have been taking it as well as he had been.

"Yeah, that's fucked-up."

"I know right," she tisked, shaking her head, "anyway, I'm gone let you go on about your day, I've gotta get started on your gender reveal!" her voice reached a high pitch in sheer excitement as the guys finally caught up to us.

"Girl." I waved her off and put my attention on Juice, who looked like he hadn't had any luck trying to pry the gender out of Eazy or Yo'Sahn.

"Can I go to TeTe's house?"

"Hell yeah, take yo lil trading ass on with them. Y'all already got my man acting funny and shit," Juice's salty ass answered before I could, giving him a light shove.

"Yeah, gone head. More crab legs for me," I sang happily, giving him a one-armed hug. It was clear that he didn't give a damn one way or the other as he shrugged out of my grip and over to my sister and Eazy.

"I don't know why you over there dancing and shit. I didn't find out what my baby is, so ain't no damn crab legs for yo ass either," Juice snapped once they'd walked off. My face instantly fell into a pout, and I froze.

"Juiiice, I been thinking bout eating since we been here!" Childishly, I stomped my foot as my stomach growled loudly, further proving how hungry I was. I hated having a taste for something and then not being able to get it, and it was that much worse since I'd gotten pregnant.

"Mannnn, get yo cry baby ass in, I was just fucking with you," he said once he saw my eyes began to glisten. Yeah, a bitch was really about to cry over some crab legs, but I didn't care. Just as soon as he relented and opened up the door for me, I'd wiped them away with a big grin. He got in, grumbling about me being phony and I couldn't even argue. I just clicked my seat belt and got comfortable as we drove away to get my food.

BUDDA

$\mathcal{J}$'d made good use of my time in the weeks since I'd robbed them hoe ass niggas. In addition to getting another car, I'd gotten me and Olivia another spot to hide out in. Since I actually had money to work with, Santos finally decided to fuck with me. I wanted to take my business elsewhere, but who the fuck was I kidding? There wasn't a nigga in the city I could trust at this point, so I wasn't taking any chances. The only reason that I even somewhat trusted Santos was because Pierre was his enemy, which made Juice and Eazy his enemies. Even if he wanted to try and snitch me out to them, it wasn't a guarantee that they'd believe him or that they wouldn't kill his ass too just for contacting them about me.

Still, Santos' loyalty would only allow him to go but so far. He'd relented and let me cop from him, but I still felt like I needed some niggas to have my back. Like I'd said, them niggas had the city on lock so finding anybody who would be willing to go against them was difficult, but I'd lucked-up. I'd been coming out of the liquor store one night and saw some little niggas on the side of the building shooting dice. Now normally I would ignore some shit like that because I had enough vices and gambling with some niggas on the street wasn't one, I wanted to pick up. What snatched my attention was the muthafucka that upped a gun. They'd already been talking shit to each other as is customary during a dice game, but lil homey took the shit a step further. With my interest piqued, I stopped to watch the scene unfold, and he definitely didn't disappoint. There was no hesitation on his part as he pulled the trigger, instantly dropping the nigga he was arguing with and sending the rest scrambling away. Unfazed, he didn't even rush as he went about snatching the money up from the ground and stuffing it in his pockets before walking off. He was a stone-cold killer, who obviously didn't give a fuck and that was just what I needed.

I was pleased to see that he didn't go very far by the time I pulled my car around the corner. He was standing outside of the gas station right up the street with a few other niggas like he hadn't just shot somebody less than a block away. Even more impressed by how little of a fuck he gave. I pulled up on them, instantly putting them on the defensive as I stepped out.

"Yo, who the fuck is you, nigga!" the original one that I was looking for, spoke with his hand on his waist. Not in the least bit worried, I held my hands up as I moved closer, hoping that would put his little trigger-happy ass at ease. It didn't.

"My name's Brian," I told him, opting not to use my street name just in case he'd heard about me. "I'm just tryna offer you an opportunity to make some cash." He regarded me with a raised brow but didn't take his hand off his gun. Up this close, I could see that he was much younger than I'd thought, but that didn't sway me though. In fact, it only made him more appealing to me and further showed why he was so quick to pull a trigger. Chicago's youth was wild, and much more reckless than back in the day, but that would only work in my favor.

"Some money... doin what?" He seemed more than a little suspicious about a random nigga pulling up on him offering him money, but that didn't kill his curiosity. They all looked like

48

they could use some extra money, and the little bit that he'd managed to snatch up off dude wasn't going to be enough for them all.

Shrugging, I stepped closer and finally put my arms down even though he still had yet to lower his defenses. "I got some work I need to get off, but I need a team of killas. Niggas that ain't scared to go to war if some shit pop-up," I told him, noting the gleam in his eyes as they all began to mumble amongst themselves.

"And what makes you think we just won't rob you? Shit, wouldn't that be more money for us?" he snorted. I hid my anger at his threat behind a smile, even though I wanted to rock this little nigga's shit. Like I'd said, these new little niggas were wild. That's what made him think it was okay to try and come at me, without knowing just how dangerous it really was. I had to remember that I was doing this for a reason, so I wouldn't put a bullet in all of their heads.

"I mean, you could, but that would still leave you out here having to rob somebody else as soon as your money got low. I'm tryna offer you the chance to be the new niggas on top. You'd have more than just some ends from a petty theft. I'm talking *big money*, the kind you can't spend in a life time, plus power and respect. That's some shit you can't get going around taking somebody else's shit."

He seemed to mull over the idea for a few seconds before finally agreeing, and that was how I'd ended up with a crew of my own. The wild one that I'd witnessed vent a nigga's head was named Bam, and along with him came Kino, Cell, Dex, Lou and Zo. They were all young as hell, between the ages of sixteen and eighteen, but I quickly found out they were really about their bread. It took them no time at all to get on their hustle and ease onto the scene, making it possible for me to go back and cop more weight from Santos.

Now, I had a steady flow of cash coming in. I'd thought I

may have had to make an example out of one of them little niggas, but they hadn't tried me yet. Since we didn't have a trap house, I was currently using me and Olivia's crib to package and distribute my shit. I wasn't dumb enough to allow any of them niggas into my crib where I laid my head, so I always met them elsewhere. After everything I'd been through with Eazy, I knew better than to trust a fucking soul, which was why I'd done some research on every last one of them. I knew where they stayed, their mama's and their grannies, and I'd put a bullet in anyone of their heads if I needed to.

"Aye, where the fuck you goin?" I asked Olivia even though I could clearly see that she was wearing her work uniform. It was early as hell in the morning, and I was sitting at our kitchen table bagging up work to take to Bam later. Every few bags, I'd cut a small amount and put it to the side for our own personal use and the pile had gotten pretty big. Her eyes fell on the coke and widened before landing on me.

"I have to go to work, Budda, I'm already late."

After looking at her closely for a few seconds, I nodded for her to go ahead and go. Besides, I liked it better when she wasn't in my face whining about stupid shit. She'd calmed down for the most part, since we'd switched up cars and gotten a place to stay. It also helped that the news wasn't showing the story on Trell anymore either. Without the fear of the police knocking down our door and dragging me off to jail, she was cool unless of course, she wanted to get high. Like now.

She'd started to walk off, but quickly backpedaled, stopping at the table and producing a straw from out of thin air. Without a word she made her a couple of lines and snorted them up, before rising back to her full height. I watched her swipe her nose clean as her body damn near vibrated from the effects of the drugs. Seeing her and knowing how freaky she got when she was high had my dick stirring in my shorts.

"You just gone bump my shit and not say nothin?" I asked, following her to the door with my eyes.

"Yep!"

The bitch must have had super powers because she flew out before I could even get up from my chair. By the time I made it to the door, she already at the car. I watched her pull away while cursing her out in my mind, but the sight across the street took my attention off of her. My eyes narrowed at the unmarked black car with tinted windows, and I hurried to slam the door shut. With my heart slamming against my chest, I peeked out of the window to see the car slowly rolling away. A part of me wanted to believe that it was one of the neighbors, but I knew it was a Fed. I was glad they'd left, I was almost certain that they'd be back though ready to cash in on my freedom. I'd just have to be gone when they did.

DREAM

"*W*hat yo fine ass in here doin?" I looked up to see Elijah entering the room, oozing sex appeal with a lopsided grin on his handsome face.

He'd been so damn quiet that I'd forgotten he was even here. Feigning irritation at the sight of him, I rolled my eyes and tried to hide the smile playing on my lips. Even though I wanted to, I couldn't deny the fact that I enjoyed having him around. He'd been doing everything he could think of to get me back, and although I wasn't giving his ass any play that hadn't done anything to stop him. Just the other day, I'd come home to find my entire living room covered in white, red, and pink rose petals with a massage table set up in place of my coffee table. The room was dimly lit with tea candles giving off a soft glow and adding to the romantic vibe. He appeared in the doorway a second after I'd arrived, dressed in black gym shorts and a wife beater as *In Between* by Dvsn started to play. Imagine my surprise when he pulled some oil from behind his back and demanded that I undress and get on the table.

I wanted to play hard, but to be honest, I needed a massage. I was stressed the fuck out between finding a new salon and

Budda still being out there somewhere. Right there in the living room, I took my clothes off, climbed my ass up on that table like he said, and let him rub my body into soft putty. I swear, Elijah put those niggas on Instagram to shame! He had me so relaxed and hot that I was ready to give him the pussy, but he surprised me by simply sending me to bed. I had to take a cold shower just to simmer my hot ass down, and days later, I was still clenching my thighs together just thinking about it.

Clearing my throat as I returned to the present, I dragged my eyes back to my laptop. "Still looking for another salon," I grumbled. Thinking about the bad luck I'd been having, instantly put me in a bad ass mood.

"Won't you take a break and come ride with me real quick." His tone told me it was more of a demand than a request, but either way, I was quick to agree. Honestly, I'd been at it for hours and hadn't found anything within my nonexistent budget, so I could use a break.

"Uhhhh, I might as well," I huffed, sitting my laptop to the side and standing, making him smirk in satisfaction.

Without a word, he waited while I slid my feet into my UGG slides and grabbed my mini back pack. Luckily, I was already dressed for the day in a pair of light-washed, distressed shorts and a black Nike cut-off hoodie. As always, he eyed me hungrily, despite the understated clothes I had on, making me simper as I passed him.

He'd been healing so good that he no longer needed a nurse. He wasn't using the wheelchair at all, which should have given me reason to send his ass back home, but like I'd said, I liked having him around. I allowed him to clasp my hand in his as we headed out the door to his car, trying to fight off the butterflies that filled my belly. My ass could fight it all I wanted, but it was apparent that I still loved this nigga.

"So, where you taking me to?" I asked as he drove with one

hand on the steering wheel and the other still holding mine. He glanced at me, flashing all thirty-two of his teeth.

"It's a surprise, so you gone have to wait till we get there." There was a gleam in his eyes that had me anxious to see what the surprise could be. I knew whatever it was, had him excited just from the way he was damn near busting at the seams. Just knowing that he was this happy to be doing something for me was making it hard as hell to stay mad at him. I bit into my lip and looked out the window at the passing cars and houses, hoping to try and control my emotions. My head was telling me to continue feeding his ass with a long-handled spoon, but my heart was swelling in my chest at every kind gesture, and I couldn't decide which one I should go with. I didn't want to let it slide what he'd done to me, but Budda had done way worse and still hadn't shown me half the love that Elijah had. I'd made so many mistakes when it came to Budda; the main one being, not leaving whenever he did me wrong. That "down ass bitch" mentality had good women out here going through it, and not getting anything in return but heartache and baggage.

I didn't want to do the same thing when it came to me and Elijah. He needed to know that there were consequences to fucking over my heart, and that just apologizing wouldn't cut it. I discreetly looked his way again as he stared straight ahead, occasionally rubbing the back of my hand with his thumb. He silently rapped along to the Roddy Ricch that was playing on the radio, seemingly content with my company, and I couldn't deny feeling the same way. Things were different with him, which I felt was further proven when he caught me looking at his ass and smiled before kissing the back of my hand, then focusing back on the road. I'd never seen a look of love so strong; it was all in the way he looked at me and in his smile. Even when he called himself being done with me; I could see that he was trying hard to suppress those feelings. Had he fucked-up by acting on impulse instead of talking to me? Yes.

Was he wrong? Definitely, but he wasn't the only one in the wrong though. I'd fucked up too by even entertaining the idea of going to see Budda, let alone actually going through with it and not letting Elijah know. If I had been honest with him from the beginning and let him know what was going on, then, we wouldn't be here right now.

Don't get me wrong, he was all the way out of order, but I also played my part in him not trusting me. Now, I had to make the decision on whether or not I was going to give him another chance or leave him alone entirely, and it wasn't much of a choice, but it was how long I was going to make him wait. I ended up getting so lost in my thoughts on our relationship that I almost didn't notice the car had stopped.

"We're here?" My brow quirked as I peeped the beauty supply store we were parked in front of, already wondering what he was up to.

"Yeah, girl. Come on." He chuckled, stepping out. As soon as I hit the sidewalk, he clasped my hand in his and led me two doors down, where Lashes and Lace was on a big ass sign outside of the building.

"Elijah, what is..." I couldn't even finish my sentence, I was so choked up.

"Look, I know there's not much a nigga can say or do to make you understand how sorry I really am. Shit, if I was you, I'd be skeptical about anything that comes out of my mouth at this point. The thing is though *I love you*, so that means that I *can't* stop until I'm back in here," he tapped my temple lightly before pressing his hand to my heart, "and in here. You deserve every piece of happiness in the world, and I'm going to do everything in my power to see that you get it. Starting with this."

By now, I was crying so hard that I had to hide my face in my hands. I just knew I looked a fucking mess standing there on the sidewalk and doing the ugly cry, but I couldn't even stop myself. This nigga had gotten me a whole fucking salon! I was speechless as he removed my hands from covering my face and placed a set of keys in them.

"Gone check it out." The grin on his face was wide and excitement shined in his eyes. He nodded for me to go ahead since my ass was still stuck in place, trying to figure out if this was real. Finally, after I still hadn't made a move yet, he took the keys from me and opened the door on his own, pulling me inside behind him.

"Ohhhh, my…." My breath was immediately taken away.

This nigga had shown out! Not only was the Lashes & Lace logo on the building, but he'd had the inside designed almost identical to our old salon. The white and chrome leather chairs had our company name stitched into them in purple and sheer white curtains separated each station. I walked further inside, taking in each one of the stations that were already stocked with everything the stylists would need. There were even mini crystal chandeliers over each one, giving them an elegant look that I could have only dreamed of.

"You like it?"

"I-I loooove it! How did you even do this?" I was busy running my hands across every surface like if I didn't touch it, it'd disappear, but I finally stopped long enough to look his way. Shrugging, he gazed at me through low eyes.

"I have my ways," he said simply, making me twist my lips in irritation. It was just like him to try and be aloof about the shit. I didn't miss the smug look he gave, knowing that he had me both amazed and curious. He was lucky that he'd already recovered for the most part, or I would have been on some "Misery" shit just to get it out of him.

"Mmmhmm." Smirking, I continued my inspection of the shop, growing more excited with each new part that I saw.

By the time I came from the back where there were two small offices—both already decorated with the same color scheme as the rest of the shop—plus a room for Destiny to do lashes in, I was smitten.

"Surprise!"

A bitch almost had a heart attack when I came out to see that Elijah had been joined by my sister, Juice, Yoshi and all of the girls who worked for us. Once again, my eyes filled with tears as they all rushed over and surrounded me.

"We back, bitch!" Destiny was the first to speak.

"Okaaaaay, and I'm so glad too, cause I was five seconds away from going to Tranique shop! Bitch, my pockets been too fucked-up!" Gabby said and everybody gave her a look.

"Really, Gabby?"

"Bitch, what? It's the truth!" Their banter had me laughing, even though a majority of the time, Gabby's ass got on my nerves, I was happy as hell to be back around her.

"So, when we opening, boss ladies?" I shared a look with Destiny, who just shrugged like it was up to me.

"Well…"

"You can open this muhfucka right now if you want, it's y'alls to do what you want to," Elijah added his two cents from the front of the room, making every set of eyes fall on him in awe, including mine. He held the keys out to me with a satisfied smirk.

"Girrrl, if you don't marry that nigga right now!" The girls all swooned just like I did, except I kept my shit together, even though I was sure he could see right through me as usual.

"I can't even lie, this was some smooth ass shit, bro." Destiny grinned with a newfound respect for him written all over her face.

"Smooth, my ass! You ain't comin back until lil Jermisha get here. So, you might as well calm down," Juice's ignorant ass just had to say.

Shocked expressions were shared between the girls, as their eyes bounced from him to Destiny. They knew of our relationships, but I'm sure it was a surprise to know that the infamous Juice had been locked down and was expecting a baby.

"Bruh, I can't take yo ass nowhere." Destiny rolled her eyes. "And you know damn well I ain't naming my baby that!"

"See, now you tryna show out, come holla at me right quick." He pushed the door open but turned once he felt that she wasn't behind him. I raised a brow at my sister waiting to see what she would do and just like expected, she stomped off after him, causing Yoshi to grumble as soon as she disappeared out of the door.

"Mann, they should've left me at home with all that lovey dovey stuff."

"Shiiiit, they look like their bouta have a lover's quarrel, to me, lil man," Elijah told him, looking out of the blinds to where Juice and Destiny had walked off to the side and away from nosy eyes.

"Nah, they always do that, be arguin one minute and kissin the next." He wrinkled his nose in disgust, making Elijah chuckle as he stepped back to give them privacy.

I chose that moment to walk over to where they stood since the girls were gossiping and popping open the bottles of champagne they'd brought. The second I was within arm's reach, he pulled me into him, and I didn't even resist. I ignored Yoshi, who groaned again and then hurried off, clearly over the PDA going on around him.

"So, am I making any progress?" Elijah's smile was a mile wide, and I had every reason to believe that it was due to the closeness between us. It was infectious though, and I found myself doing the same.

"You're doin a lil something." I shrugged jokingly, pinching my fingers together for emphasis.

The truth was that *this* was probably the biggest gesture he could've done for me. It damn sure meant the most! Him going out of his way like this, while he was going through so much spoke volumes, and my heart was swelling in my chest despite my modest reply.

"Oh, this a *lil something,* huh?" He grabbed my chin softly and brought his face so close to mine that we were almost kissing. "You ain't seen shit, shorty," he promised with a smirk.

ELIJAH

*B*etween trying to win Dream back, searching for Budda, and still trying to recoup the money that nigga had stolen, I had little to no time to deal with my family issues. Honestly, I was just using all that shit as an excuse to keep me busy, so I wouldn't have to. In a matter of months, I'd lost my mama, Trell, almost lost my brother, and my own life had come close to being snatched away. As if that wasn't enough, I had to find out from the nigga, who put me on, that my father wasn't really my father. I was fucked-up, but holding it together well enough that nobody noticed, and if they did, they didn't say anything. Which was the way I liked it. I would deal with Pierre on my own time, and Big E too. I'd been ignoring all of my pops' calls because I didn't know what I wanted to say to him. I couldn't be mad about the shit because he'd stepped up and taken on another nigga's job, but at the same time, I felt like he should have said *something*. It made me wonder what he would've done had Pierre not come up to the hospital. Would he have explained to me why the fuck his blood didn't match my own or would he have continued to lie to me?

I shook my head and tried to get my mind on the issue at

hand, which was the fact that I'd recently been losing foot soldiers. Common sense told me it had everything to do with Budda, who'd declared war by his actions, but I still needed to investigate. We were about to have a meeting, so that I could figure out who knew what. Something blocking the sun, had me reaching for my waist, only to come face-to-face with Juice's ugly ass.

"Nigga, I don't know what you reachin for. If I was an opp, you would've already been gone," he fussed as soon as I rolled the window down. As usual, he was puffing on a blunt. Instead of me getting on his ass about it like I would have done before, I reached out and snatched it from his hand.

"Yeah, Aight, ain't another muhfucka bouta catch me slippin." I took a couple of deep pulls and allowed the smoke to seep out of my nose before attempting to give it back.

"Nah, keep that shit," Juice quickly declined with his face frowned-up. "All that ass kissing you been doin to Dream, ain't no tellin where yo lips ain't been."

I laughed as I cut the ignition and climbed out. Little did he know that Dream wasn't fucking with me like that, no matter what I did. I called myself trying to win her back on some noble shit, so the day I'd massaged her soft ass body, it took everything in me not to dip in that pussy. I figured it would work out better for me in the long run, and now, I was seeing that wasn't the case. Dream had a moment of weakness that night; I could see it in her eyes, but she'd quickly gotten over that shit. Even after gifting her the new shop, she'd still been keeping me at arm's length, but I definitely wasn't giving up until she was mine again. I walked with Juice into the trap, finishing the rest of his blunt on the way and throwing it just before we ducked inside the door.

Upon seeing us, the twenty niggas we had working for us, all stood at attention with the five from this particular house standing in front. Juice eased over to the right and sat down on the arm of the burgundy couch while I paced the open floor, stopping right in front of Quin, the house's lieutenant.

"Who we missin, Quin?" I questioned, watching him closely to make sure he didn't lie. I already knew that there were six that just up and disappeared, but the fact that he'd waited a damn week to say something had me looking at him funny.

Clearing his throat, he let his eyes wander before meeting my hard stare. "Six, man....Lil Mikey, Trey, Red, Yung, Bk and Jazz." I shared a look with Juice, who merely shook his head. Somebody was definitely knocking off our runners; regular Chicago violence usually alluded us. Not saying that we were untouchable, but out of all the years I'd been running shit, I could count on one hand how many times my niggas got killed over some beef shit. Now, all of a sudden, six muhfuckas were dead in the span of a week? The shit didn't sit right with me.

"Why the fuck I'm just now hearing about this shit!" I vexed, growing more heated as I spoke. I didn't know if the weed Juice had was trash or what, but it definitely wasn't calming me down.

"I thought I could handle it." He swallowed hard and looked up at me meekly as I chuckled.

"You thought? This nigga *thought* he could handle *my* shit!" I repeated angrily. Without warning, I went across his shit and felt his nose crack under my fist. Like the G he was, he stumbled but didn't fall, knowing that his punishment would be much worse if he showed weakness. With a sniff, he swiped his nose, checking for blood before lifting his chin in the air. "You can't handle shit! If you could, then six muhfuckas wouldn't be dead right now!"

I eyed the rest of them niggas, daring anyone of them to step up and say something, but they all just looked straight ahead. Somebody had to have heard or seen some shit that would help me the fuck out, and I was prepared to fuck with their livelihood if I didn't hear shit.

"Y'all better put y'all fuckin heads together and tell me something, or I'm hitting y'all pockets around this bitch!" my voice boomed off the walls, making them grumble.

I saw movement out of the corner of my eye and turned to see Benzo, the lieutenant of another house, raising his hand in the air.

"Nigga, what the fuck you raisin yo hand for? This ain't school," Juice cracked from across the room, gaining a few chuckles that died down instantly once I set my steely gaze on the group.

"You bouta tell me something useful, B, or you gone say some shit that's gone make me fuck you up?" I asked, pinching the bridge of my nose as I waited for whatever he was about to come out of his mouth with.

"It's some new niggas out here with stepped-on work. One of the fiends told me yesterday when he came to cop. I ain't think nothin of it cause it's always somebody tryna come around sellin fucked up shit, but he said the dude name was Bam."

"Bam? The muhfucka that be robbin niggas?" somebody voiced quizzically. "I ain't never heard of him slangin, but I wouldn't put it past him to try and sell some shit he stole."

"See, now y'all niggas thinkin. Find that his ass and bring him to me."

"I'm gone keep it a buck, E, that nigga a loose cannon. He liable to go out in a blaze of glory before he let us get anywhere near him."

With narrowed eyes, I stepped in his direction. "Well, I guess, y'all better make sure he don't get the chance to, then. Meeting adjourned."

* * *

AN HOUR LATER, I'D DROPPED JUICE'S ANNOYING ASS OFF AND was on my way to handle some other business. I had yet to address the shit storm that Sherice had caused since I had so much other shit going on, and I wasn't sure if her disappearing was due to her actually being pregnant or because her ass was lying. After all of her stunts, it seemed like she'd crawled under a rock or some shit, and I hadn't heard from her. I was gone be the one popping up, today. Parking my car across the street from her condo, I cut off my lights and sat up, so I could get a good look at her crib. Her bedroom light was the only one on, letting me know that she was still up, so I shot her a quick text.

Me: you up?

I watched as the little bubbles appeared on the screen a second later, giving away how thirsty she was.

Sherice: Yes daddy, you wanna come over?

I damn near choked on my spit while reading her response. I didn't know if the bitch had confused me with another nigga or her actual daddy, but she had to know I wasn't fucking with her like that. For the sake of my mission, I decided to play along.

Me: hell yeah, I'm twenty minutes out.

Sherice: Ok, I'm ready baby.

Shorty was laying it on thick with the pet names, and I could only imagine how she was running around, trying to set shit up for me. The meme with bitches washing up in the bathroom sink crossed my mind, and I shook my head with a chuckle. My laughter was cut short by her front door opening and a half-dressed nigga, with a pregnant belly came stumbling out, shouting obscenities. Sherice appeared behind him, tossing what I assumed was the rest of his shit out, completely unfazed by his threats. Though the sight before me was hilarious, I wasn't trying to be out there all night. I put in a FaceTime call to Dream and waited patiently until her pretty face popped up on my screen.

"Yes, Elijah?" Although her tone was fake annoyed, the smile on her face let me know she was happy about me calling.

The sound of chatter and a view of her work station behind her told me she was at the shop, which was probably another reason for her smiling. Ever since I'd given her those damn keys, she'd been in that salon. I was happy to be the one to bless her with that, although with her determination, it would've only been a matter of time before she'd gotten it on her own. Finally having her business back had removed the stress from her eyes, and she was much more cheerful and upbeat.

Like a love-struck teenager, I smiled, seemingly put in a better mood just from seeing her. "Don't be answering like a nigga buggin yo ass or somethin," I teased, loving the way she playfully rolled her eyes and simpered.

"Maybe you *are* buggin me, sir."

"Nah, I don't even believe that, and you don't either."

By now, the old man had gotten the hint and walked off, cursing as he made it to the Cadillac that was parked in front of me. I kept my eyes on him until he pulled away from the curb, before bringing my attention back to Dream.

"Aye, do me a favor and go somewhere private."

The request was met with raised brows, sensing that I was up to something. She looked around to make sure nobody else heard me before standing. "I'm goin to the back real quick, y'all." Dream was already moving as she spoke, instantly causing a chorus of whoops and hollers from the stylists; all of them teasing because they knew I was on the phone.

"I hope you had me come back here for a reason," was the first thing out of her mouth once she'd closed herself to her office.

"Everything I do is for a reason, shorty," I said confidently just as I knocked on Sherice's door. Dream didn't get a chance to respond because as if she was already standing on the other side, Sherice swung the door open and tried to pose sexily.

"Heyyy, you," she purred.

I could vaguely hear Dream going off as I slowly advanced on Sherice, trying my hardest not to wrap my hands around her throat. Her expression immediately became one of fear after seeing the look in my eyes, and she continued to back farther into her apartment.

"Dream, didn't I just tell you it's a reason for everything I do?" I finally addressed her, looking down into her angry face. She was hot!

"Oh, I know damn well you ain't come over here with that bitch on the phone!" Sherice, who'd suddenly found her voice, had stopped moving and was standing before me with her hands on her hips like she had a reason to be mad.

"I got yo bitch, you bum ass hoe!" Dream countered. Now, they were going back and forth, yelling threats and insults at each other.

"Aye! Shut the fuck up!" my voice boomed, silencing them both, even though I was only talking to Sherice's dumb ass. With my hard stare still on her, I spoke directly to Dream, hoping to calm her mean ass down long enough for me to explain. "Dream, you know I ain't tryna do nothin to disrespect you or fuck up the progress we've made, but in order for us to get anywhere, you need to know that I have no ties to this bitch."

"I don't need to know shit about *her*."

"But I need you to," I stressed. "Can you honestly say right now if she's pregnant, for real, that you'd give a nigga a real shot?" I already knew the answer to that without her even having to say. Hell naw, she wouldn't! Probably one of the biggest reasons that she was curving me so hard was because of Sherice's lying ass telling her about a baby that I knew, for a fact didn't exist. My point was proven when she looked off silently, unable to lie and say that she would.

"Exactly, and I can't be mad about that cause I'm the reason you even have these reservations, but I'm also gone clear shit up when I need to, so we can get back right."

"Y'all really bouta sit here talkin bout me like I ain't here?" I ignored Sherice's tantrum and focused on my girl, whose face showed her exasperation with this whole thing.

"Fine, Elijah," she huffed, rolling her eyes.

A mischievous smirk formed on my face for two reasons. One being that Dream actually *wanted* to give me a chance to fix things, which meant that she still had hope and two, because I was about to enjoy this shit more than she knew. With a wink, I pulled my gun out of the waistband of my joggers, holding it in a way that only allowed Sherice to see it, making her eyes grow wide.

"Good. Now, Sherice, bring yo ass over here and tell my girl the truth." I beckoned her towards me with the gun that she hadn't stopped gawking at. I paid no attention to Dream sucking her teeth at me saying she was my girl, as I watched Sherice tip toe in my direction. She'd have to get used to that shit because as far as I was concerned, she was mine.

"E-Eazy—"

"Aht, talk to her, don't speak to me." Turning the camera so that Dream could see her now tear-filled face, I nodded for her to go ahead.

"Dream," she dragged out her name slowly. "I'm *not* pregnant okay! Elijah made me take two fucking Plan Bs right after we had sex. There was never a baby! Tuh! You happy now?"

"Yep! You lucky I don't go get shorty right now and have her stomp yo ass through this floor, but the truth is enough for now. Just make sure you remember that I can always come back, Sherice. Go on bout yo life with yo johns and leave me and mine alone." The realization that I knew about her little side hustle had her face frozen, but I didn't even stick around. My business with that hoe was complete. Tucking my piece back down into my pants, I walked out, not even closing the door behind me.

"I can't believe you just did that, nigga." Dream chuckled, shaking her head.

"Shiiit, I don't know why not. I'm doin any and everything I can for you, baby, believe that." I wasn't lying either; whatever I needed to do to ease her mind, I would, even shit she didn't know she wanted or needed. Dream and Eazy were going to be back, better than ever.

JUICE

*S*ince things had somewhat returned to normal, I'd been taking Yo'Sahn to the Y with us. Even as young and short as he was, he was still balling with our grown asses like he was over six feet. I could tell that all of this shit was hard for him. Constantly having family and friends succumbing to the street life was bound to take a toll. Our roles in his life had been to prevent shit like that, but it seemed like it was only getting worse with our presence. A huge part of me felt guilty as fuck about all the chaos we'd brought, but Destiny was constantly trying to remind me of all the good me and Eazy had done too. That didn't really make me feel any less guilty though. Spending one-on-one time with him did kind of help, but I was always over cautious because of the shooting at the school.

"Man, that lil nigga a ringer or some shit!" Ant muttered, draining his water bottle.

"Don't be mad yo ass can't play! My baby girl probably gone come out the pussy with more game than you, nigga!" I cracked and took a seat next to him on the bleachers. We'd only played one game, and we were already winded and needed a break, but Yo'Sahn and Chad were still going.

"Fuck you, Juice! That's why I hope you fuck around and have a boy," was his only comeback, but little did he know, I really didn't care what the baby was. I wanted a girl, but the only reason I said the shit so much was because it clearly bugged the fuck out of Destiny, and after a while, it just became a habit.

Shrugging, I told him just that, only making his cry baby ass grumble more. I tuned him out and focused on Yo'Sahn as he hit a smooth three-pointer, touching nothing but net. My boy was a beast on the court, for sure. I could definitely see his little ass going pro if that's what he wanted to do.

Chad was out there clowning, running around, and mimicking a cheering crowd with his hands cupped over his mouth and shit, making Yo'Sahn laugh as he fought to catch his breath. They slapped fives and then made their way over to where we were sitting. Yo'Sahn plopped down right in front of me, and I handed him his bottle of Gatorade since he'd worked up a sweat and clearly needed it.

"Lil homie got game, bro." Chad nodded in approval like he was telling me some shit I didn't know.

"On God," I agreed, roughly rubbing the top of them lil adolescent dreads Yo'Sahn loved so much. Just like expected, he ducked out from under my hand and attempted to smooth his ponytail back down.

"Come on, Juice, man." The scowl on his face reminded me of his mama, and I had to laugh. They looked just alike when they were mad. It had me wondering if my baby would come out looking like a mini version of her, and I couldn't wait to see.

"I don't know what you whining about, them lil shits too short to mess up!" I teased, reaching for them again, only for him to swat my hand away.

"The shorties at my school fuck with em, though," he said with his chest puffed out. We all laughed at his little over confident ass.

"Tell yo mama bout the shorty's at yo school, and she gone beat yo lil ass!" That instantly shut him down and turned the cocky grin on his face into a mean mug. Destiny didn't play that shit, and he knew it.

"Man, you always gotta bring my mama into it!" he grumbled.

"That's my trump card!" I shrugged, still laughing. "Don't hate the playa."

"You ain't shit, Juice, let lil man rock," Ant's lame ass chimed in like he hadn't just been talking shit a few minutes before.

"Nigga, you was just—never mind. I'm gone holla at y'all niggas later. I need to get him to the crib." I shook up with them both before standing to my feet and tapping Yo'Sahn.

"Aight, bro. Stay up, lil man."

"Peace. Tell Eazy to bring his cripple ass too, next time," Chad said, slapping hands with Yo'Sahn. I nodded that I would, as me and my lil homie left. With his ball tucked under one arm and his phone in the other hand, he walked beside me through the front lobby, barely looking to see where he was going.

"Heeeey, Juice!" a couple of hoes from around the way crooned as we passed them. On some cool shit, I shot them a head nod and kept on about my business, not even bothering to give them a second look. I didn't need to see them to know they didn't have shit on my girl, pregnant or not. It had me shaking my head at how quickly Destiny's mean ass had changed me.

If somebody would've told me six months ago that I'd be damn near married with a baby on the way and a step son that I'd risk my life for, I would've laughed in their face. I guess it was true t, when they said that you'd change for who you wanted to. Destiny had definitely changed my wild ass for the better, and I couldn't deny that. The fact that Yo'Sahn barely even batted an eye at them hoes being thirsty for my attention, let me know that he trusted me. It felt good to know that he had faith in me when it came to his mama, and I was gone make sure to keep his trust.

We'd been riding for a good twenty minutes when he turned down the volume on the Roddy Rich, I was blasting. I could already tell that he had a lot on his mind from the way he was tossing his ball around and staring out of the window the whole ride. Usually, he'd be rapping along animatedly and jumping around to the point where I'd be ready to put his little ass out. Today, he was quiet as a church mouse.

"Aye, Juice," he finally said once he'd gotten his thoughts together. "My birthday comin up right. So, I was wondering if I'm gone have to spend it with you and my mama, or am I gone have to go to Antonio's house?"

Without meaning to, I felt my face instantly ball up. We'd had enough conversations about his bitch ass daddy for me to know that spending time with him was the last thing he wanted to do, let alone on his birthday. The question was why in the fuck did he feel like that was an option. Looking between him and the road, I lifted a brow and asked. "What makes you ask that?"

He shrugged his shoulders and continued to play around with his ball. "I don't know, he was already talkin like I'd be living over there and shit, then I saw this paper talkin about custody and stuff in my mama purse. On TV, that's how they do that shit right? Sometimes, the dad gets the kid and sometimes the mama do?"

I was blindsided by all this shit, so it took me a minute to even process what he was saying. Destiny hadn't said anything to me about no custody papers, which was a problem in itself. The way she was acting over the nigga sending a social worker out, I could only imagine how stressed she was behind some actual court documents. She hadn't been walking around acting like she was pressed about it, and I was sure that she was gone try and handle it on her own. I gripped the steering wheel tightly and tried not to express how pissed I was, even though I was fuming. Knowing how much Yo'Sahn meant to his mama, I was ready to dead that nigga, Antonio.

"Is that what you want tho? Cause if not, then I put it on my life you ain't gotta ever see that nigga," I vowed, turning to him as we stopped at a red light.

The last time that he'd pulled some fuck shit, me and Destiny were both dealing with those dumb ass detectives, but since Eazy killed Dre at the club, the police had to drop it. As far as they knew, Dre had been the one to kill his own damn granny. It definitely made sense after the way he rolled up on my brother, but I really didn't care as long as it exonerated us.

"Hell, naw! I mean, it ain't like he messed with me before. He can stay where he at, for all I care," Yo'Sahn spat. I knew that he rarely let his emotions show and always tried to be hard because that was just how shit went for young men out here. You had to grow up faster, especially when you were being raised by a single mother. I was here now, and I would go above and beyond to take care of them.

"Bet. You ain't got shit to worry about, then," was my reply as I stuck my fist out, which he pounded, solidifying his unspoken trust that I'd make something happen.

After that, nothing else needed to be said and his mood seemed to lift immediately. He cut the radio back up and was done with the conversation since his mind had been put at ease, but now my shit was running wild. I kept it cool though, and even stopped to grab us some chicken sandwiches from Popeyes before we headed back home.

When we got there, he greeted his mama, who was sitting on the couch feeding my baby, before running off to shower. I waited until he was out of the room and sat down right next to her, slipping my arm around her shoulders. After dropping a kiss to her cheek, I snatched up a few of the fries from her plate and stuffed them all in my mouth.

"Got dammit, Juice! Don't be putting yo nasty ass hands in my food!" she immediately started fussing, like she was mad about me touching her shit, but I knew it was really because I'd taken some from her greedy ass.

Ignoring the pout on her face, I pulled her closer and kissed her again. "Stop acting like you ain't happy a nigga home and give me a real kiss. That last one tasted like a nasty attitude."

"I swear to God, yo ass is crazy." She sucked her teeth but did as I said, puckering up her lips. I devoured them, quickly sucking them into my mouth and biting them lightly until she moaned, getting excited herself. Instead of deepening the kiss like I'm sure she wanted me to, I pulled back. "Why you stop?" Her pout was back in full effect.

"Why you ain't tell me that nigga had papers drawn up for Yo'Sahn?" I countered, making sure my voice was low. She froze up, shock instantly replacing the annoyance that had just covered her face.

"How do you even know about that? You been goin through my shit?" She tried to get up from the sofa but was slowed down by her belly, which had grown even more. Using her little setback to my advantage, I wrapped my arms around her waist and pulled her onto my lap gently.

"Don't try and flip this on me, shorty, all that other shit irrelevant. Why you ain't tell me? We supposed to be in this shit together and you keeping secrets."

The more I spoke, the more mad I got, just thinking about it. Lowkey, a nigga's feelings were hurt that she'd kept something like that from me and had possibly been stressing my daughter out while worrying about it on her own. Sighing, Destiny set her plate down on the coffee table and then got comfortable in my lap, turning so that her feet were now on the couch with us.

"I'm sorry… I'm just used to taking care of things on my own when it comes to Yoshi. Plus, you had so much other shit on your plate I—"

"And I already told you, that you and Yo'Sahn are my responsibility now. I don't give a fuck what I got goin on, I'll drop all that shit for y'all. That's what a real man does. I know Dre and yo bitch ass baby daddy got you feelin like you gotta handle shit on yo own, but I ain't nothin like them lame ass niggas. Any problem you got automatically becomes *my* problem, and I'll take care of it for the both of us, but you gotta trust me," I said, lifting her head so that she could look at me.

It fucked with my mental to see the doubt in her eyes, and I wished that I could bring Dre back to life just to kill his ass myself for making her feel like she couldn't count on anybody besides herself. Since I couldn't get ahold of him, I'd make sure to make Antonio's ass pay for his part.

"Say you trust me," I ordered, giving her lips a peck.

With a heavy sigh like a nigga was getting on her nerves, she draped her arms around my neck. "I trust you, Juice."

"Bet, now believe it, cause I got you." I looked directly into her eyes, so she knew how serious I was. When she nodded, I kissed her again. I knew she was still hesitant, but I would just have to show her better than telling her. Breaking my lips away from hers, I tapped her lightly on the butt. "Aight, go get that paper, quick, so I can see it."

Instead of arguing and putting up a fight like she normally would have, she went and did as I asked, letting me know off rip that she was trying. Now, all I had to do was keep my word and look out. Like I'd told her, they were my responsibility now— my family—and I'd always make sure they were straight.

BUDDA

Olivia wasn't happy about having to leave our apartment, but I wasn't taking any chances. At this point, I didn't know what those grimy ass Feds would do if I didn't give them something on Eazy and Juice. Not to mention, I wasn't even where I'd planned on being money wise. Shit had quickly spiraled out of control, and I had no clue what I could do besides continue to lay low.

Constant paranoia had my mind running a mile a minute, worrying about both Eazy and the Feds. At this point, I was ready to straight flee, but the measly money I had on hand damn sure wasn't enough to start over somewhere, plus I still had Olivia to consider. I didn't trust her to not snitch on me and try to save herself, which was why I rarely let her leave my side. Her little habit was another way that I'd managed to keep her under my thumb, but the move had her highly alerted to the fact that something had happened. I'd considered killing her and just being done with it, but I couldn't shake feeling like she'd be useful to me at some point. I hoped that wasn't in vain though.

"Aye, come suck my dick right quick," I ordered from my spot on the bed as she tried to walk by after her shower.

The sight of her wet body wrapped up in a towel had my dick hard, even with the little bit of weight she'd lost from the drugs. Knowing that she'd be ready to do anything with a little motivation, I held up a small baggy, quieting any argument she was about to raise. I leered at her as she came over and dropped to her knees before me. Dumping the contents of the baggy onto my bare thigh, I watched her snort it up excitedly. Just thinking about her throat game had my dick strain even harder against the thin fabric of my boxers. Once there was nothing left but residue, she licked that up too before setting her eyes on my hard dick. I'd already freed it by now and was stroking it, waiting for her to get to work. She quickly replaced my hand with hers and began sucking on the tip, which she knew I loved. The bitch may have been brain dead, but she could suck a cough drop through a straw. She'd barely gotten started and already precum was oozing out in anticipation.

"Fuck!" I hissed when she swallowed my shit whole, making sure to gag.

Saliva dripped from her mouth down my shaft and covered her hands when she inched it back out. Up until now, I'd been clenching the hotel's cheap ass bedspread, but I couldn't take her playing with me. I grabbed a fistful of her curly hair and fucked her face hard, lifting my ass off of the mattress as I got more into it. My toes cracked and curled as I felt my nut shoot out and coat her mouth and throat. I wiped the sweat from my forehead and released my hold on her as I fell back on the bed, trying to catch my breath, but she wasn't done. Loosening the towel she was wrapped up in, Olivia climbed into my lap, not even bothering to remove my boxers. She grinded against my semi-hard dick, bringing it back to life before slipping it inside of her tight hole.

"Ooooh damnnn, Budda!" she squealed as she rocked against me, squeezing her pussy muscles so tight that I felt like my dick was in a chokehold. I held onto her waist, trying to slow her down since I was damn near ready to bust again, but when she started bouncing on my shit, it was over.

"Gah damn, girl! I'm bouta nut!" I gritted, gnashing my teeth together.

"Meeee tooooo!"

She did some shit that had her whole-body vibrating, and I was shooting off once again. Breathing heavily, she fell on top of me trying to cuddle and shit, but I shoved her away. What was meant to be a quickie on the head side had turned into a whole session, and I was late meeting up with Bam and the rest of them little niggas. Ignoring her sucking her teeth, I hopped up and went to wash my ass again. After a quick shower, I came out and slipped into another pair of boxers and some jean shorts before slapping Olivia, who was still laying there on her bare ass.

"Get up and take a shower, so we can go."

She grumbled and stormed off to the bathroom, slamming the door behind her. If I wasn't so pressed for time, I'd beat her ass, but I decided to let her slide. God was either working on me, or he was looking out for her dumb ass. I grabbed a plain, black pocket tee out and threw it on, not really caring too much about how I looked since we wouldn't be out long. I'd barely put my feet into my shoes, and Olivia was already strolling out of the bathroom in one of the dingy ass towels. With narrowed eyes, I watched her step into a pair of thongs and then pull on a flowing sundress.

"What now, Budda?" she questioned without even looking at me. I guess, she could feel my gaze on her as she moved about the room.

"Bitch, that quick ass shower! Did you even use any fuckin soap or did you just let the water run on yo dirty ass!" I was waiting on her to lie, so I could slap the taste out her mouth. Being with a woman, you know that whatever fruity ass soap lingers in the air when they come out the shower. I'd smelt it the first time, but this time there wasn't shit but the hotel soap filling the air from my shower, plus it'd only taken her like two or three minutes, tops.

"I swear, you find something to fuss about every damn day! I used the hotel soap since I just got out, it wasn't no need to be in there no long ass time!" Waving me off, she continued to get ready. I chuckled irritably and checked the time on my watch. I was more than a half hour late, and I wasn't trying to argue with her. It was her pussy, if she wanted to go outside smelling like budussy then that was on her ass.

"Whatever bruh, just hurry the fuck up." I finished putting on my shoes and snatched the keys, up so I could wait for her dumb ass in the car.

Almost an hour later, I was pulling up outside of the building that Bam insisted we meet at, even though none of his friends or him lived there. I left Olivia in the car and met him on the curb, with my eyes peeled for any bullshit. Regular summertime Chi had niggas and bitches galore out on the street, and I wanted to make sure none of them paid me any mind.

"Nigga, you late as fuck for a meeting *you* called. Now, I'm late for some other shit!" he sneered as soon as I was within earshot.

"I got held up. Where the fuck everybody else at though?" I'd wanted to meet with all them niggas not just his ass. That's how I knew this drug shit wasn't their thing. When the boss says meet up, that's what the fuck you do. Wild asses didn't even know how to follow directions!

His brows bunched to his forehead at my question obviously confused. "Why would them niggas be here? You texted me for a meet up."

"It don't matter, who I texted! All y'all niggas was supposed to come when I said it was a meeting!" I fumed, raising my voice angrily and drawing a few stares. "Y'all muhfuckas need to get on the same page."

"Aye, I know you feeling a way, but you better pipe the fuck down, bruh. I ain't yo child to be out here yelling and shit." His tone was calm, but there was an icy edge to it that had me taking a step back and lowering my tone.

"My bad," I told him, holding my hands up in surrender. I knew that I had to play it cool with his ass. He was still the same nigga I'd witnessed kill somebody in front of a crowd of people just to go in his pockets. "I should've told y'all......just, next time I say it's a meeting you know everybody's supposed to be there, unless I say only you." I could tell he wasn't feeling me still, but he nodded his understanding.

I waited a second before speaking again to see if he was going to say something, but he continued to look at me blankly. I assumed he was waiting for me to get to the point of this meeting, so I did.

"Aight, so I really just had you come because y'all niggas movin too reckless. You can't be out here killin the competition's crew. That's gone draw a lot of unnecessary attention to us, and we not ready to go to war yet if it comes to that."

Last, week he had mentioned to me that they'd had to kill a couple of foot soldiers out west. I automatically knew he was talking about niggas from Eazy's camp because he ran that shit out there. A couple wouldn't have been an issue, but these niggas had actually killed six! That was too much for it to be a coincidence, and I started to tell them to just lay low for a while, but then they might've wanted to know why. That's why I figured a meeting to tell them to slow down would be better.

"What you mean attention? Ain't nobody said *shit* to me, not even when I did the shit! Them niggas know what's up and didn't you say them Mexican niggas got our backs if shit go left?" he questioned eyeballing me. I swear, I could've kicked my own ass because all of my lies were catching up to me. I'd told him that, but Santos wanted no parts of my beef. All he was willing to do was make money with me and as fast as he had sold to me, he'd be selling to the next dumb ass nigga.

"Uh yeah, they do, but we still need a bigger group than just us seven! We ain't even got a spot of our own out here! Look, it just makes sense to have our shit solidified. The goal in this shit is to make money, not war. I know y'all niggas used to doin whatever, but you gotta have a lil more discipline in this game," I tried to drop some gems on him.

"Oh, so you sayin it's like rules to this shit?" he quizzed with a grin like he'd just discovered some shit.

"Yeah, that's *exactly* what I'm sayin."

"Aight, I get it, like don't get high off yo own shit too, right." He nodded, wiping my proud smile right off my face. "Yeah, you and yo girl lookin like y'all one hit away from rehab, nigga. Get that shit together and let me worry bout this street shit." His jovial look was gone and replaced with a sneer as he pointed to my nose, before stalking off. Self-consciously, I swiped the tip of my nose just in case there was some residue there and sure enough, there was. Shaking my head, I stormed back to the car with an attitude. This arrangement clearly had a shelf life, and I wanted to get as much money as I could before shit went south.

DESTINY

"*B*itch, didn't Juice tell yo ass not to be in here working with that belly?" Dream teased as soon as I stepped foot into the new shop. I flipped her off and spoke to everyone else before taking a seat in Ashley's chair.

"Juice don't *tell* me shit! He's this baby's daddy, not mine!" I said smartly, rolling my neck extra hard.

"Mmmhmm, oh shit! There he go!"

I immediately went into escape mode, ducking down into my seat and ready to take off, but at the sound of the girls laughing at me, I sat up and hit all their ass with a mean mug. "That shit wasn't funny, y'all petty bitches."

"Oh yeah, it was!" Dream was laughing so hard; she was holding stomach. "You should've saw your face!"

"Yeah, you was definitely scared as hell! I don't blame you though, everybody know yo nigga crazy. I probably would've been running right behind yo ass!" Gabby added, slapping hands with Sariah, who was already nodding in agreement.

"Ain't nobody scared of that nigga." Even with that lie rolling off my tongue, I still hadn't gotten my heart to slow it's pace as I discreetly glanced at the doorway. I could talk a good game, but

Juice had been serious when he said he wanted me to wait until the baby came to go back to work. He made sure to pay for anything I wanted or needed, and he was at my every beck and call just so I'd stay my ass at home. Yo'Sahn was even in on it, calling himself snitching if I even looked like I was trying to come here. The only reason I was able to sneak away today was because I actually needed my hair done, and neither of them were willing to sit here and wait for me to finish. As soon as he gave me the okay, I shot out of there fast as hell. I had an appointment with Ashley, but I had also scheduled two clients myself. Sure, I was trying to learn to trust Juice to handle things, but I was still a hardworking mama. He couldn't just expect me to quit cold turkey.

"Don't nobody believe that lie but you, boo." Dream's bald-headed ass was on a roll trying to crack jokes and shit. The bitch swore she was a comedian. I bet she wouldn't find it funny if I told Eazy she was taking niggas' numbers. Sticking my tongue out at her, I got comfortable in my chair and sat back, so Ashley could take down the two French braids I'd put in my hair after washing it.

It felt good as hell to have our salon back, even though I'd only been inside of it twice since we'd reopened. I couldn't wait to get back to work and be whipping bitches' eyebrows and lashes. It had me excited just thinking about it. Especially, since I'd been stuck in the house unable to think about anything besides the sex of the baby and Antonio trying to take me to court. No matter what Juice said, it was hard not to worry about that too. The least he could do was let me come back to work to take my mind off of it, but that was too much like right.

"So, what you want, girl?" Ashley questioned as she ran her fingers through my hair. The shit was feeling so good, I was just about ready to take a nap, and with my full stomach, it was only a matter of time if she didn't stop. *Damn, baby.*

"I was thinkin a high ponytail."

"Oooh that's gone be cute on you!" I shook out the twenty-two-inch bundles I'd brought with me and handed them to her. She didn't have to tell me, I already knew I was gonna slay, baby bump and all.

"Thank you," I gushed with a wide grin. She got right to work and since I'd already taken the liberty of washing my hair at home, it cut the time in half. While she busied herself on my head, I tuned in to the shop gossip. Even though we'd just opened, a lot of our old clients had already been making their way back. Not to mention, the few that we gained after opening up next door to a beauty supply.

"So Dream, finish tellin us about yo date," Danielle put my sister on the spot, never taking her eyes off of the feed-in braids she was doing. The rest of the girls chimed in, wanting to know themselves.

"Ooh yeah, what Eazy romantic ass surprise you with now?"

"I bet it was good!"

Dream was blushing and trying to bite back her smile, but that Eazy glow was all over her. If I didn't know any better, I'd swear she'd given in and gave up the draws. I couldn't say that I'd blame her because buying another shop was some next level shit.

"It was *not* a date," she lied with her head down as if she was really focused on her client, but I knew she was only trying to hide the truth in her face.

"Then what was it a booty call, cause that'd be even better!" Gabby's nosy ass said.

"See, now, you already know I ain't bouta do all that." Dream was right back in business mode once the conversation took a turn to raunchy. Even before Eazy, she was never the type to tell another bitch too much of her business, but she was even more private now, and she definitely didn't like it done in front of customers.

I chuckled as they all let out sounds of disappointment. I

knew for sure I'd find out later, but I couldn't say the same for them. Everybody got back to other topics of conversation as the bell over the door went off. All eyes fell on Makalah, and I instantly turned up my nose. Even my baby started kicking, like she just knew a hoe had stepped in the vicinity. *Dammit, Juice!* He even had me calling the baby a girl. That thought had my attitude through the roof.

"Aht, aht. Didn't you see the sign? We don't service hoes!" I growled before I could stop myself. She seemed surprised to see me, and she threw her hands up defensively.

"I didn't even come here for all that, I just saw a new shop and wanted to check it out."

"Ok, well you came, you saw, you got treated, now you can go." She was already backing away, but I leaned forward acting like I was about to jump up from my seat, giving her a glimpse of my belly in the fitted t-shirt, I was wearing. Her eyes widened when they landed on my stomach, but she knew better than to even ask me what she already knew.

"Damn girl, is you deaf and dumb! Get yo ass up outta here!" Sariah hissed, making her snap out of her trance and rush out of the door. Dream wasted no time grilling the both of us, but I just shrugged and sat back so that Ashley could finish my hair. "My bad, boss lady, but ole girl's face was upsetting me and my home girls."

Sariah had everybody in the shop cracked up laughing as she continued to roast Makalah. I was laughing my ass off to her doing a re-enactment of the scene that had just happened when my phone went off on my lap. Seeing Juice's contact had me sucking my teeth in irritation.

"Booooy, what yo ass want?" I started giving him straight attitude before the FaceTime call could even connect good. His handsome face popped up twisted in a mean mug as usual.

"Don't answer the phone like that? I'm calling to check and make sure you ain't indulging in no ratchet ass behavior while my daughter with you." He took in as much of my surroundings as he could through the camera, seeming to relax just a bit when he saw Ashley moving about behind me.

"Nigga, you tried it! Ain't nobody doin shit, *Jeremiah.*" Sometimes, I had to just roll my eyes at his ass. He was always doing the most. I hadn't realized it, but a hush had fallen over the salon as everybody tuned in to my conversation.

"Yeah, Aight, you better act like you know before I come up there and fuck up the half of yo head that's done," he threatened with a smirk. I couldn't stand his scxy ass! I looked up to see the heffas hanging onto my every word.

"Uh, uh see, you got all these thots up in here drooling and shit now." I narrowed my eyes at them as I spoke, and they all busied themselves even though I knew they were still listening.

"Yeah, but you the only thot I want drooling on this dick though," he said with a straight face.

"Bye, Juice!" I didn't even wait for his mannish ass to respond as I hung up right in his face while Dream and everybody else busted out laughing. A second later, my phone was chiming in my hand from a text, and I knew it was him.

Bae: You know you payin for that when you get home, right?

Not bothering to reply, I blacked out my screen and finished getting my hair done with a smirk on my face. The way my hormones were set up, I was anticipating him putting that foul mouth on me already.

A few hours later, I was walking through my front door, swinging my ponytail extra hard. As soon as Ashley finished whipping me up, my first client arrived, and by the time I was done with her, the other one was waiting to be done. My ass was thirsty to get home and see what Juice had in store for me. He must have heard me pulling up because before I could slam the door shut behind myself, he was coming around the corner. Dressed casually in only dark gray basketball shorts and black

Nike slides, he puffed on his blunt as he looked me over in appreciation.

"Bring yo hardheaded ass here and let me feel them lips." He beckoned me with a head nod, and I switched right over, not even giving him a smart response like I normally would. When I was close enough, he pulled me into him with one arm while putting the other behind his back to keep the smoke from his blunt out of my face.

I moaned when our lips locked, loving how he could handle me with such care, but be rough at the same time. As usual, Juice grabbed a handful of my ass. I pressed closer to him, easily growing more aroused at the feeling of his hard dick. I could already feel a puddle growing between my legs, when he pulled away.

"Juuuice!" I was ready to beg for the D, and he was just standing there with a sexy ass smirk on his face.

"I told you, you was gone pay for hanging up on me, didn't I? Besides, yo sneaky ass think you slick. I know you was up there workin. This lil ponytail shit cute, but it ain't take no four hours." He gave my weave a light tug, as I opened and closed my mouth, unable to argue the truth. "Nope, don't lie, just bring yo ass on and get in the tub before yo water get cold."

He let me walk ahead of him to our bedroom, smacking my ass on the way. When we got in the bathroom, he immediately went to check the water's temperature while I stripped out of my clothes. Once again, I got salty after he helped me into the tub of hot water, only to order me to wash while he left the room. After he hadn't returned ten minutes later, I washed my body a couple of times before cutting on the shower and washing twice more.

By now, I was mad because I knew at some point tonight, he was going to leave, and I had yet to receive my backbreaking orgasm that I needed before bed. I shot him an evil look as he sat on our bed, comfortably browsing through Netflix. Dropping my towel dramatically, I went about the room collecting one of his tank tops from the dresser. I could feel his eyes on me as I sat down on my side of the bed and applied my Brazilian Bum Bum cream to my body, paying special attention to my growing stomach. I always made sure to keep my give a little extra attention there, so I could keep the stretch marks at bay. Lord knows I loved my kids, but I didn't want no war wounds. As soon as I was done and ready to lay down, Juice spun me around and placed my feet in his lap.

"We Netflix and chilling tonight, since the lil homie with Pops," he said, gripping my foot in one hand and palming my belly with the other. Just like the spoiled brat he or she was, they began kicking, causing him to give me a cheesy grin. "See, even baby girl wanna kick it with daddy, don't you?" What I really wanted to do was slide my pussy on his face, but I guess I'd have to settle for a movie night instead.

"Fine, Juice, but don't pick nothin stupid," I huffed.

"It's whatever you want." With a shrug, he tossed me the remote and began rubbing my feet. They'd already begun to get a little swollen from my standing today, but I wasn't gone tell him that. I could barely keep my attitude or work the remote with the way his hands felt on me. He pushed his thumb up the arch of my foot, and my hot ass almost came. With the way I was moaning, you'd have thought he had me bent over.

"Mmm, that feels soooo good!" I cooed, throwing my head back.

"You can cut all that shit out cause I'm still not fuckin you. Yo ass on dick punishment for hanging up on me. Now, pick a movie before I do." I swear, this nigga knew me so well. As good as his foot rub felt, I'd definitely been putting in on an attempt to entice him, but he'd seen right through that shit. Rolling my eyes, I began looking for something to watch while he grinned, proud of himself for whatever reason. It was okay; he won tonight, but I knew he wouldn't be able to hold out too long.

DREAM

"You know, you don't gotta come up here every night to walk me to my car." I was speaking to Eazy, but my eyes were on the safe as I filled it with the day's profits. As usual, he was sitting in one of the chairs in my office while I finished things up.

"What you tryna get rid of me or something?" Even though I knew he was teasing, I still stopped what I was doing to give him a hard stare, which he gave right back.

"Yeah, so my new nigga can pull up." I laughed, but Elijah didn't.

"He gone be pullin off in an ambulance." His face was dead ass serious, and I hurried to turn around and finish what I was doing. As sweet as he was, he'd definitely changed since his mama had passed, and I could believe that if a nigga pulled up, he would make good on his threat. That was one of the main reasons why I had been trying to keep my little texting buddy a secret. It wasn't anything serious, just a guy I'd met while grabbing my morning coffee. He was cute and didn't appear to be anything like the thug ass niggas I'd surrounded myself with in my last two relationships, so I'd taken his number. I ended up using it one night on some bored shit, and we'd been having conversations ever since. It wasn't going to go any farther than those texts, despite how hard he'd tried to see me again in person. I was bored, not crazy. Besides, Elijah was still staying at my house even though his home had been completely fixed after Sherice had gone and fucked it up. I had no intentions on sending him away either. As long as he wanted to stay there, he could. Well, at least until they found Budda.

"I was just joking, Elijah, don't nobody want my ass but you," I tried to lighten the mood since the vibe had changed drastically after my last comment.

"Plenty niggas want you, Dream, but ain't nobody gone *have* you but me. Not even that lame you call yo'self hiding."

Oh shit!

The chill in his tone had me both scared and turned on at the same damn time. I didn't know whether I should jump in his lap or run the fuck up out of there, but I played it cool. "I'm not *hiding* anybody. We're not together, and I can talk to who I want t—" Before I could even finish my sentence, he was behind me, yanking my frail ass up and into his hard chest.

"Say it! Say you can talk to who you want to. Any nigga even think about getting close to you, and he's disappearing. I put that on my mama's grave. The only reason Cordell ain't seen me yet is because you're smart enough to know not to do shit but text that nigga," he gritted, literally reading the entire situation. The fact that he knew Cordell's name proved that I wasn't nearly as slick as I thought I was. Swallowing the lump in my throat and unable to lie, I asked the question that was burning me up.

"How did you know abou—have you been going through my phone?" My fear was quickly replaced by anger at his audacity.

How dare he go looking through my shit, especially after what he'd done. He was the last person that needed to be acting like his trust had been betrayed... again. For the first time during the conversation, he laughed cockily before lowering his face to mine.

"I don't gotta go through yo phone to find out shit about you. That's bitch nigga shit. The more important question is why you playin with that man's life? Especially, when you know you wanna be with me."

I opened and closed my mouth, stupidly. Not wanting to admit that what he was saying was true, but I also wasn't trying to deny it either. The truth was that as much as I wanted to be with Elijah, I wasn't ready to let my guard down with him just yet. I didn't want to feel like I was doing the same things all over again, even though he was far from the man in my past.

Seeing me struggling with my words, Eazy shook his head and blew out a frustrated breath. "I see, I gotta take a more *hands-on* approach with you. Take off your clothes." The command came with so much authority that for a brief second, I started to do so.

"Wha—what?" I stuttered as he stepped back and leaned against my desk, giving me just enough room to do what he'd demanded.

"Take. Off. Your. Clothes." With lowered lids, his eyes roamed my body as he spoke each word slowly and deliberately.

Even though my heart was finding it difficult to accept Elijah back with open arms, my pussy had no problems in that area. In fact, at the moment she was crying for him, and he hadn't even touched me yet.

"I don't think that's a good idea—"

"Why, because you know that once you physically give in to me, it'll be hard for you to keep denying the truth?" he cut me off with that same cocky tone.

"No, but—" My words got caught in my throat as he pulled me to him by the hem of my shirt and pressed his lips against mine.

As our tongues connected, I could feel his hardness pressing against me where I stood between his legs, making any of the fight I had, leave my body. It had been a hot little minute since I'd had some dick. My vibrator, though handy, did not compare to anything that Elijah could do. I felt his cheeks hike into a pleased grin when I got more into the kiss, wrapping my arms around his neck with a moan as he squeezed my ass in both of his large hands. Smoothly, he lifted me off of my feet and had my skirt pushed up around my hips. The seat of my panties were so wet I could wring them out, and my clit jumped from anticipation as he sat me on top of my desk. He only broke our kiss after removing his gun from his waistband and sat it beside me before dropping into my chair and scooting all the way up, until he was eye level with my center.

"Sssss, ahhh!" I whimpered, arching my back as soon as he pushed my panties to the side and his lips latched onto my clit. He sloppily licked me from top to bottom, holding me in place by my thighs to prevent me from running.

"Sit yo ass still, Dream, I'm tryna clean my plate." He looked up at me as he spoke with his beard glistening. Again, he buried his face in my wetness hungrily, grunting and smacking like he was eating the best meal he'd ever had.

"Ohhh, God damn!" Grabbing ahold of my desk for support, I trembled violently, unable to control my body from the effects of the orgasm that tore through me. I was still shaking and trying to get my breathing under control, but Elijah didn't stop until he pulled another mind-numbing eruption out of me. Still spent, and with loose limbs, I was too weak to move when he slid me off of my desk. With my legs hanging on each side of him, he sat me right on his awaiting dick, filling me right up.

"Mmmm."

"Damn, I missed this, baby," he admitted, holding me tightly without moving as we both relished in the feel of each other.

My pussy fit him snuggly, and I couldn't deny I missed it too. I nestled lower, squeezing my muscles around him as I did, before positioning myself so that my feet touched the floor, giving me more leverage to move. Without missing a beat, Elijah freed my breasts from the tank top, suckling the left before giving his attention to the right one while I rolled my hips on top of him.

"That feels sooooo good, baby." Moaning, I bit into my lip and tried to keep my rhythm with the added stimulation of his hands roaming my body and his oral attack on my neck and chest. His hot tongue was trailing a blaze everywhere it landed, driving me crazy.

"I know it do, cause this *my* pussy, Dream. You understand?" he grunted, grabbing the back of my neck and forcing me to look into his eyes as he pumped into me. I don't know how, but he was hitting every spot and that shit was even more intense because of the heavy eye contact.

"Yesssss! Yes! I dooo." He licked his lips sexily as he looked down between us, watching himself stroke me, before bringing those hooded eyes back to me.

"Good. You better tell that lame too!" His eyes narrowed, and he began delivering lethal blows, that literally had me immobile. "This my shit, just like this dick belong to you!"

"O-ok, I'm bouta cum, Eazy, shit!"

"You so fuckin wet! Gone head let me feel it, baby!" he urged, and just like that, I was cumming for the third time, jerking involuntarily and falling against him. "I'm right behind you, I'm bouta nut all up in my pussy, Dream, can I?" His pace quickened as he spoke, letting me know that he was close to the edge.

"Mmm, yes!" Pressing my lips against his neck and planting light kisses there, I squeezed my muscles, milking him of every drop of semen he had while he growled lowly. I could still feel him throbbing inside of me as he shoved his tongue in my mouth, and I eagerly accepted it.

"You know I'm dead ass serious about everything I just said, right?" he asked as soon as he caught his breath. "That wasn't just no sex talk. I'm done playing with yo ass."

I waited for a sign as we stared at each other; something solid to let me know if giving Elijah another chance was what I should do because I felt like I couldn't trust myself in that moment. I was straight up dickmatized and in love with his ass already. Making a decision while we were still connected physically seemed more emotional than rational, but I couldn't help how I felt. There was no denying that I missed and wanted to be with him, so I made up my mind right then that I would.

"You better be, Elijah King, because if you hurt me again, I'm going to be done, and there won't be no coming back," I told him, meaning every word.

"That's something you don't even gotta worry about. I'll hurt my damn self before I do *anything* to have you doubting my word again." His promise was followed up by another kiss, before he pulled back slightly. "Now, let that nigga know right now, then block his ass," he said, producing my phone out of thin air and shoving it into my hands. I couldn't even do shit but laugh as I did what he asked.

JUICE

"*And* you sat there while she texted that nigga?" I questioned, looking at Eazy in disbelief.

He'd just finished telling me about how he finally had broken Dream down to give his sorry ass another chance. I'd been telling him for a minute that he was gone have to stop all that overly exaggerated simp shit and just tell her what it was, just like I'd done her sister. I was glad that he'd finally listened, and the shit had been squashed because all that wining and dining shit was starting to make Destiny look at me like I was slipping. I did what I could, but romance wasn't my damn strong suit. This was my first time ever being in anything close to a relationship, and I'd gone straight from boyfriend to baby daddy fast as hell. I did nice things for my girl though; I rubbed her fat ass feet, brought her food all the time, I'd even ran bath water for her. It was no doubt she appreciated everything a nigga did, but I could see that she also liked to see her sister getting flowers and shit. My hood ass didn't even know where to get some damn flowers from though.

"Hell yeah, I did! It was either that or go tell his ass myself," Eazy said with an unbothered shrug. I could see that a weight had been lifted off of his shoulders since he had his girl back, but I was still gone fuck with him.

"Yo soft ass! You dangerously in love nigga?" Cackling, I looked between him and the road, making him frown irritably.

"Is you? I mean, you the one bouta fight a nigga."

"Ain't gone be no fight, my man just gone take this ass whoopin and get the fuck on," I asserted, and now, it was Eazy's turn to laugh.

"Either way, yo ass bouta fight to prove yo love!" This nigga was cracking the fuck up like he wasn't going along for the ride.

"Man, fuck you!" was the only response I could think of because the truth was, my ass was going to fight a nigga to prove my love.

We were currently on the way to Antonio's mama's house, so I could do just that. If Destiny knew what I was on, she'd probably have a fit thinking that it would fuck up her chances in court, but I was sure that this was just what she needed to get rid of this nigga. He'd been asking for it ever since he brought his dusty ass up to the hospital when me and Yo'Sahn had been shot, and he'd gotten way too many passes. Nobody was going to be stressing my bitch out or threatening to take what I now considered a son, away.

We pulled up to the small house not too much later, and since it was fairly late, the block was still. His car sat right out front just like I knew it would cause his lame ass didn't have no business about himself. He wanted Destiny to believe that he had a chance in hell of snatching her son away, but the nigga still stayed with his mama. Besides her social security, the only income in the house that they could use was his girlfriend's, who worked at some sleezy ass strip club. Even knowing all this and being positive that my lawyer would demolish this nigga in court, I still felt like it was important that I personally see him.

"You just gone knock on the door, huh?" Eazy teased as we walked the short distance to the porch.

"Yep." I was already in go mode, so him giggling like a bitch beside me didn't bother me at all. As soon as my foot reached the porch, I was beating on the door like the police before a raid, and I didn't let up until it swung open and an angry old lady stood, glaring at me.

"What the hell—Hey get outta my house!" she shouted at my back since I was already inside and making my way through like I owned that bitch.

"Sit yo old ass down!" I heard Eazy tell her while I continued my search.

The first bedroom must've been hers because it looked like an old lady's room, and it was empty, just like the next one and the bathroom. When I approached the last room in the hall, I pulled my gun even though I had no intention on using it.

"Who y'all niggas lookin for! It ain't shit back there!"

I ignored the lie she'd just told and kicked the door open to see Antonio asleep on his back with a chick beside him. Without warning I brought the butt of my gun down onto his stomach, instantly making him jump up with a groan.

"Arghh, what the fuck!" The sudden movement caused his bitch to wake up, screaming as she clutched the sheet around her chest.

"What's up, Ant?" I flashed him a quick grin and tapped his face with the gun still in my hand. "Get yo ass up and come holla at me."

"Holla at you? Nigga, what the fuck you doin in my house!" He tried to sound tough in front of ole girl, like his ass wasn't literally on the brink of pissing on himself.

"I'm tryna give you a fair one, but if you don't get the fuck up, I'm just gone beat yo ass right here in front of yo bitch. What it's gone be?" Truthfully, he was gone catch a fade either way, but at least if he got up, he'd have a chance to look like a man. I glanced down at my watch in the dark to emphasize that his time to decide was running out, as his girl looked between the two of us with wide eyes.

"Aight, then..." I shrugged, cocking back.

"Okay, okay!" He threw his hands up and swung his legs out of the bed quickly, despite the obvious pain he still felt in his abdomen. I stepped back to give him some space to slip into his sweats and some shoes while he tried to plead his case, but I wasn't trying to hear that shit.

"Ant, you ain't really bouta leave with this crazy ass nigga?" his girl asked, watching helplessly from her spot on the bed.

"Just-just stay up in here, aight." He straightened his spine, and with a chuckle, I motioned for his bitch ass to go ahead of me. There was no way I was turning my back on him. Reluctantly, he made his way out of the room, walking like he was heading down the green mile and shit.

"You really got this nigga up like this an after school fight!" Eazy shook his head as we came up the hallway, clearly amused. At the sight of my brother, Antonio quickly tried to turn around, but I pushed him back towards the living room.

"Antonio, what did you do! Got these niggas in my house and shit!" The old lady looked stressed the fuck out by our presence, but I wasn't leaving until I beat her son's ass.

"It's cool, mama," he grumbled as we walked by, waving for her to stay seated when she tried to stand up.

Eazy's funny looking ass was right behind us the second we stepped outside, and he made sure to close the door behind him. I handed him my gun, ignoring the smirk on his face and hopped off of the porch after Antonio.

"Look, man, what's this about? I hope it ain't got shit to do with Destiny's shit starting ass."

Once again, he started trying to plead his case even though nothing that he said was going to stop me from fucking him up. I threw my fist up, and with the quickness of a professional boxer, I hit him with a right and tried to knock his jaw loose.

"Awww man, fuck!" he howled, grabbing his face in agony. "What the fuck! I wasn't even ready yet!"

He'd barely gotten the words out before I was sending another mouth shot his way that knocked him on his ass. "You better get ready, then nigga!"

He looked up at me angrily from his spot on the ground before standing up and spitting out the mouthful of blood he had. Getting into a fighting stance of his own, he threw a weak punch that I easily dodged and came back with a combo, making him stumble backwards. I guess, now he was big mad because when he finally shook off his daze, he did the normal bitch nigga shit and tried to rush me. We locked up with each other because he wasn't strong enough to make me fall over.

"Nigga, I ain't tryna be here all night while y'all muhfuckas hug!" Eazy talked shit from the porch.

"Man, fuck you!" I grunted, pushing Antonio off of me.

"Fuck you getting mad at me for? Stop playing with his ass and finish this shit."

Just like I did, Eazy knew that this was a quick win for me. I could've ended this shit with my first punch, but I wanted to beat this nigga's ass, and I wanted him to know why. Tired of wrestling, I lifted him off his feet and slammed him to the ground, hard enough that I knew his shit was going to be hurting for days.

"Move the fuck around, ain't shit to see here!" Eazy barked at a group of kids that had slowed down as they walked by, trying to record us.

I didn't even look their way, once I had Antonio on the ground unmoving, I yanked him up by his shirt. Dazed as fuck, it took him a minute to make eye contact, but when he finally did his face was bitter.

"Bring me my gun," I spoke, without turning away, and Eazy came down handing my shit over.

Even though I knew the nigga was scared, he still tried to put on a brave face as I held it under his chin threateningly. "You already know this fade was because of Destiny and because I heard you were talkin shit while I was laid up in the hospital, but *this*," I jutted my chin towards the gun, "this is because you tryna disrupt my family. Truthfully, I should just splatter yo shit across this lawn, but I'm gone give you a pass because at the end of the day, you're Yo'Sahn's daddy, regardless of how absent you been. And maybe he might want a relationship with you at some point. That's gone be up to him and his mama though, not you. So, when this court date come up, you gone walk yo bitch ass up in there and tell them that you made a mistake and Yo'Sahn belongs with his mama, or else I'm gone come back and kill you, yo mama, and yo bitch. You got me?" He nodded vigorously as I shoved the gun deeper into his flesh. "Speak the fuck up, nigga!"

"Aight! Aight! I'll tell em that he should stay with Destiny!"

"Good, now you make sure you keep yo word cause if it ain't shit I hate worse than a deadbeat, but a deadbeat ass liar," I chided, smirking at him evilly before standing to my feet and tucking my gun away.

He didn't make a move to get up as me and Eazy walked off like nothing had happened. If he knew what was good for him, he'd do what the fuck I'd said. I wasn't playing about coming back and killing the whole house, if they had a dog, I'd kill that bitch too! Wasn't shit off limits when it came to niggas coming for my family, no matter how big or small.

"You feel better now since you got that out yo system?" Easy prodded as soon as we were back in the car and headed home. He couldn't even keep his amusement off of his face.

"You act like I just did that for nothin. The nigga tryna take lil homie away." I could feel my face tightening from how irritated I was. Sure, a lot of that had to do with Antonio thinking he could say and do whatever he wanted to Destiny, but I still needed him to understand that taking her son wasn't an option.

"Nigga, you know damn well they wasn't bout give him shit!" he argued with a laugh. "Yo ass just wanted a reason!"

I couldn't even fight him on that cause I knew the shit was the truth. I'd gotten Destiny the best family attorney that money could buy, and with her income and proof that she'd been taking care of Yo'Sahn alone all these years, she was sure to win. The ass whooping wasn't necessary in regard to the case, but it was needed and long overdue.

"Well, if he don't do what the fuck I said, then that lil fade gone be the least of his worries!" I admonished cause I damn sure planned on airing that bitch out if he said anything other than what I'd told him to.

"You already in step daddy mode."

"You muhfuckin right! Top flight step daddy of the world, nigga!" Me impersonating Day-Day had us both laughing, but I was serious. I'd stepped up with the whole family thing, and I wasn't about to fuck it up.

EAZY

*D*ays later, and I was still laughing about how sprung Juice was over Destiny. I knew dude ass had it coming though for trying to insert himself into Yo'Sahn's life after all this time. The whole reason we'd even crossed paths was because he wanted to help his mama pay bills, since that nigga wasn't doing his part, and neither was her so-called man. I shook my head, thinking back on how that one encounter had changed our lives for the better, before checking to make sure the safety was off on my gun and climbing out of my truck.

The opening of my club had been completely shut down after that shit that Dre had pulled. I was pissed about all of the money I was out, but there wasn't shit that I could do. At this point, the only option was to sell and try to recoup something, though it was going to be much less with all of the damages. Today, I was meeting with a potential buyer, and I was hoping that I'd be able to get it taken off my hands.

As soon as I stepped into the building, I got pissed off just seeing how bad it looked. Although I'd explained to the woman over the phone what happened, I knew that picturing something and actually seeing it were two different things, and she might very well run or give me a low-ball number.

"Hey, Elijah, I wasn't sure you'd make it. I was just showing Mr. Blackman around," my realtor, James, said with a huge smile as he walked from the back.

Any pleasantries I might've came back with got swallowed down at the sight of Pierre and his security. I hadn't seen his ass since he came over to Dream's house wanting to clear the air, and it hadn't been by accident. He'd told me if I wanted to talk to call, but yet, he'd been the one calling me for the last couple of days. I bit back on my molars and tried to keep my anger from showing since James wasn't aware of my street side. As far as he was concerned, I was an ordinary business man, and that was how I wanted to keep it. Instead of pulling my gun like I wanted to, I shook hands with James and regarded Pierre with a stone face.

"James, I can take it from here." No further explanation was needed since I was sure he'd read the tension in the room.

"Uh, well it was nice meeting you, Mr. Blackman. I look forward to doing business with you." He shook Pierre's hand and nodded my way uncomfortably.

"Likewise," was all that Pierre gave him, never taking his eyes off of me. A second later, he was gone, and I finally decided to speak.

"What the fuck you doin here?" I sneered, no longer masking my true feelings. I hadn't been in a rush to consider his offer of a relationship because as far as I was concerned, we could leave it like it was. There wasn't anything he could do for me, besides continue to supply us. I already had a father, despite being kind of pissed at him at the moment.

Pierre sniffed arrogantly and swiped his nose before speaking. "You might not like the situation we're in, Eazy, but don't forget who the fuck I am. I been letting you slide with the slick remarks because I know you feel some type of way, however, it's only so much disrespect that I'll take."

"Nothin you just said answered the question of why the fuck you here, though," I ignored his threat, completely unbothered. If Pierre didn't know shit else, he knew that I wasn't afraid of him in the least, and it wasn't because of his new updated status as my sperm donor. I didn't bow to anybody, and I damn sure wasn't about to start with him.

"I guess, I can't knock you for the very same traits that connect us." He smirked with a shake of his head, then continued when I didn't acknowledge his comparison. "I've been trying to get in contact with you because I found out some information that may be useful. Since you've been ignoring me like I'm some bothersome female, I figured a different tactic was in order."

"Oh, we got an early shipment or something, cause that's the most useful shit you could tell me. If not, then we can cut this short. I got way more important shit to do with my time." That was only a half-truth. I did need to stop by my house and check to make sure things were to my liking since they'd finally finished fixing it, but it wasn't necessarily important. I was just mad about the potential buyer actually being him. In my mind, that was lost money and wasted time.

"I know where this new team is that's been killin off yo people," he threw out, stopping my departure mid-stride. Turning to face him, I tried not to give away my piqued interest in what he'd said, but I definitely wanted to know. Despite the threat of losing money, my guys had yet to bring me the nigga, Bam, or anyone from his camp. In fact, I'd lost three more people, and I was just ready to end this shit.

Seeing that he had my attention, a pleased look crossed his face as he continued, "So, I do know something of value then?"

"It's as beneficial to you as it is for me and Juice to take down

Budda. Don't act like you doin us any favors. If you know where the fuck them niggas at, then tell me, so we can go handle it."

"True, but you have a personal vendetta against him." He shrugged. "My only concern is the money he stole, which is still more your problem than mine. However, the fatherly thing to do would be to help you in this instance."

"The most fatherly thing you ever did was let the man who raised me, be my father. If you gone tell me, then do that and stop with all this other shit." I was tired of going back and forth with him. He was acting like this shit was a game and treating it like a drug deal, instead of the life or death situation that it was.

"Look, Eazy, I'm not the deadbeat you're painting me out to be, and I can explain my side if you'll give me a chance. I just want you to know that I did what I felt was best, at the time. Despite it all, I stand by my decision, knowing that it aided in the man you've become." Even though I wasn't trying to have this conversation right now I couldn't deny the sincerity on his face. "That's all I'll say for now, but I'd appreciate you hearing me out one day soon." I nodded that I would and slightly relaxed. I'd had a great life with Elijah King, and if Pierre removing himself from the equation had made that possible, then I couldn't really be angry. Like he said, that was a conversation for another day though.

"Aight, I'll give you that, now can we get to the matter of Bam and his crew of idiots?" I questioned with my brows raised. I was anxious to get at them niggas. The faster we were able to dead this shit, the faster we'd be back to business as usual. A grin spread across his face, and I couldn't tell whether it was from me agreeing to talk to him or because he knew some niggas were about to die until he spoke again.

"Aye, Bruno, go get the car. I'm riding with you, it's been a minute since I got my hands dirty."

* * *

I DIDN'T MIND PIERRE COMING, BUT I MADE IT CLEAR THAT JUICE was bringing his ass too. So, we stopped on the way to pick him up. Of course, his goofy ass was confused as fuck about what was going on and why I was with Pierre, but all I told him was that we had a location. We did a drive-by of the house that Bam was supposed to be holed up in, and I couldn't even lie, the shit looked abandoned. It had me side-eyeing Pierre's old ass, like maybe he had the wrong information, but at the same time, him staying in such a rundown ass place had made it possible for him to hide from my men. The block was busy as fuck at this time of day; full of kids playing and shit. The car slowed down a bit when we started to pass a group of niggas standing around on the corner.

"That's the nigga you been looking for." Pierre nodded out of the window. "The one in blue." As soon as he spoke, Juice started reaching for his gun, but I quickly stopped him.

"Not now, bro."

"The fuck? Why not, the nigga right there." Juice was visibly irritated as he screwed-up his face at me. We were both ready for this shit to be over, but I wasn't willing to risk innocent lives just to catch him.

"It's kids and shit out here, man, that nigga liable to start shooting just to get away. I know you not tryna have no dead shorties on yo conscience," I reasoned, looking at him sternly. He grumbled, pissed that I was right as we pulled away while Pierre looked on in silent approval. "We gone come back later tonight, after we change and get a different car, but don't trip, we gone get his ass."

Hours later, when the sun had finally set, we were back, and the block had quieted way down. Surprisingly, there wasn't even any niggas out. It seemed like everybody had gone inside like they already knew shit was about to go down. We parked in the alley and left the hooptie running while we crept up to the back door.

I'd convinced Pierre's old ass to stay back, so me and Juice could handle this shit alone, and the only reason he'd agreed was because I promised him a piece of Budda. He was delusional as fuck if he thought I'd bring him along. I'd try the father-son shit, but like he'd said, this was personal and considering that me and Juice had lost the most, we should have been the first up for revenge.

We made it to the door, and I listened intently for any signs of movement inside, but all I could hear was the sound of a TV. I didn't want to make too much noise kicking the door down, so I motioned for Juice to pick the lock. We didn't know what we were walking in on, so we had to be careful. Lucky for us, the door only had a knob and not a deadbolt, making it as simple as sliding a card through the slot. A second later, we were in and creeping through the dark kitchen. The only light was coming from a room in the hall that looked to be a bathroom. I almost threw up in my mouth from the smell of what had to be the pile of dirty dishes everywhere. This nigga had to have roaches with the way his kitchen looked, alone, and I'd only seen what little the light covered. With Juice behind me, I inched further inside and my feet instantly started sticking to some shit on the floor, making me move slower so that no one would hear it. Juice cursed under his breath, and I knew that he'd stepped in the same shit I had, but before I could shoot him a warning look over my shoulder, a figure emerged from one of the rooms. The nigga, Bam, stepped into the hallway carrying a bowl, ready to put it amongst all of the other filthy ass dishes, until he saw us. His eyes widened in shock, and he dropped that shit as he took off to the front of the house. Without hesitation, I fired a silent shot that hit him in the back of his leg, dropping him just as he reached the living room.

"Arrgh!" he yelled loud as fuck while me and Juice searched the rest of the house for anybody else, but he was there alone. What we did find though was a few bags from the mall and some of the work he'd been trying to sell. I carried the baggies to the living room with me, where Juice was already waiting with all the lights now on.

"Nigga, what the fuck you cut all these lights on for?" I huffed, showing him the work that was in my hand.

"It's dark as hell in here! We already stepped in some shit in the damn kitchen. Wasn't no telling what else was in this nasty muhfucka. I ain't tryna take no roaches home with me, bruh, I heard they run when you cut the lights on." The shit he was saying was comical as hell, but the look on his face was dead serious. I couldn't even say shit because I'd had the same thought about this nigga having roaches.

"Yo ass slow, man," I told him, shaking my head before walking over to where Bam laid on the floor, still moaning and groaning. "Who the fuck gave you this shit to sell?" He glanced at the drugs and scoffed like I was playing with him.

"Nigga, fuck you! You gone kill me anyway!" he said through clenched teeth, eyes blazing angrily.

"You right, I am," I affirmed with a nod. "But at least the nigga who got you into this shit will meet the same fate, instead of walking around spending the money you earned with no repercussions."

"Do what you gotta do, I ain't no fuckin snitch!" Disappointed but not surprised, I sighed. The little nigga definitely had heart, too bad his loyalty was to Budda's bitch ass.

"Man, gone feed this muhfucka a bullet, so we can get the hell up outta this dirty ass house!" Bam gave Juice an icy glare from the insult. "What you lookin at me for? You know this shit nasty. I outta shoot you just for that."

"Fuck you too, bitch ass nig—" His sentence was cut off by a bullet lodging in between his eyes. Him and Juice would've gone back and forth all night if I let them, and we ain't have time for that shit. I left him there on the floor, leaking and went in search of anything that could lead me to Budda. It didn't take long to find his phone and with that and the drugs in-hand, we left the apartment the same way we'd entered.

BUDDA

*I*t had been a couple of weeks since I'd talked to Bam, and I could only assume his little reckless ass was dead because if he was in jail, I'm sure he would've been blowing me up. Considering how he was out here living, there was no telling what had happened to him or who had done it. Since he was the only one I kept contact with, I couldn't call and find out shit, and I was obviously vexed. I needed to pick up my money because the stays in these hotels were becoming expensive, and my cash flow was dwindling. Hanging up the phone from yet another failed attempt at reaching him, I sat my phone down and wiped my ass before flushing the toilet. I was so damn nervous that my stomach had been fucking with me bad, and I always had the urge to shit. Between hiding from the Feds and Eazy, I hadn't even had time to think of a plan to get Dream, and as more time passed, I figured she was the least of my worries. All a nigga had wanted to do was come home, claim my spot back, and get my bitch back with me, but shit had been going all wrong.

I shook my head and made my way out of the bathroom to see Olivia's coked-out ass still sleeping. It was one in the afternoon, and she still hadn't even so much as rolled over yet. She was one of the worst mistakes I'd made. Since I'd been out, I'd turned her into a dependent ass crackhead, and I was honestly over it. She was more of a liability than anything, and I was about to cut my losses with her. Frowning at her still frame that was twisted under the sheets, I went about the room getting dressed. If Bam didn't want to answer the phone, I still knew where he lived, unbeknownst to him, and I was just going to pop-up on his ass. I still had two packs left to try and get more money, plus whatever they'd come up with.

Half-dressed in only my jeans and shoes, I grabbed up the small bag I kept my work in, needing to check and make sure it was still there for some reason. Like I said, I was extremely paranoid and didn't have time for anything to throw me off. When I opened it up, I saw only some crumpled-up bills at the bottom amongst loose powder. Angrily, I shoved the bag aside and stormed over to the bed ready to kill this bitch.

"Olivia! Get the fuck up!" I snapped, punching her in the face to wake her, but she didn't budge. Growing more vexed by the second, I yanked her up by the thin t-shirt she wore and hit her a couple more times, only to realize that she still wasn't moving. With squinted eyes, I leaned in close before dropping her back on the bed. "Bitch, why you dead!"

I watched her body slump against the headboard and backed away quickly. This bitch was really dead! In a hotel room that we'd been in together, with drugs! I frantically looked around the room for nothing in particular, just stuck trying to figure out what the hell had happened. The thought to beat her dead ass ran through my mind briefly, but just as quickly went away. My eyes landed on the paper lying on her nightstand that I hadn't paid any attention to until now. I snatched it up, damn near ripping it.

Bryan, I just can't live like this anymore. I'm tired of running and constantly looking over my shoulder, but mostly I'm tired of you. It's because of you that I'm on drugs and can barely recognize myself when I look in the mirror. I hope Eazy finds you and shoots you in the dick, bitch! Rot in hell! Oh, and no need to look for your drugs, I snorted most of it and dumped the rest.

Olivia

"Arrgh, you stupid bitch!" Fuming, I grabbed her limp body and shook her, wishing that I could bring her ass back from the dead just to kill her again.

I didn't even give a fuck about her being dead; she could've jumped her silly ass off the top of the building for all I cared. The fact that she'd disposed of my only source of income was my biggest issue, besides her killing herself in our room where I had prints all over! I really wanted to believe that she hadn't done that stupid shit, but here I was with a dead body and no drugs inside of a hotel room.

Not wanting to waste any time, I went around and tried to wipe my finger prints off of as many surfaces as I could, before snatching up all of my things and throwing them inside of the bag that my drugs were once in. Shit, I even grabbed the note just so there wouldn't be shit tying me to this room. Since it was in her name, the only thing that could connect me to this bitch was if they found any of my DNA, but even then, that didn't mean I'd done anything to her. Throwing on my shirt, I used the hem of it to open the door, making sure to wipe the knob as thoroughly as I could as I left the room. It was paid up for another day, so that gave me a twenty-four-hour head start as long as none of the nosy ass housekeepers took their asses in there.

I took the stairs, instead of the elevator and tried to hide my face from the numerous cameras that were around. This shit had me wishing that I'd stuck to the rundown ass motels where they definitely wouldn't have come to the room for shit, and I could've avoided being caught on camera. All of this shit was running through my mind as I made my way to the car, grateful that I at least had that to fall back on.

I made it to Bam's raggedy ass house in record time and as usual, his block was buzzing with activity, but I didn't even give a fuck. I double-parked on the street and hopped out, shooting a daring look at anybody that looked my way. The way I was feeling, at the moment, I'd set it off right now with whoever wanted it. They must have sensed my mood because they didn't say shit as I walked by. I pounded on the door like the police and waited, growing more pissed off as time passed with no answer.

"Hey, you lookin for Bam?" some bitch asked from the porch next door, and I had to bite back my smart reply because it was obvious, who I was looking for.

"Uh yeah. You seen him?" I could already tell that she was only trying to spark up conversation with me from the look in her eye. She was sizing me up, damn near drooling, but I didn't have shit for her. Bitches hadn't brought me shit but trouble lately, and although her fine ass was just my type, I was in survival mode. She stood up on the stoop, I'm guessing to give me a view of her body as she grinned sexily.

"Naw, I ain't seen him in like a week. I think his bad ass moved or something. You his people?"

"Kreshia, take yo smut ass in the house! Out here being thirsty and shit! I'm tellin mama!" one of the little niggas out there blasted her, making her flush in embarrassment.

"Shut up, Lil Kev! You ain't my damn daddy!" she shouted, giving away how young she was. If it hadn't been for dude calling her out, I would've sworn she was grown. At this point, I knew I needed to get the fuck out of there. Turning my back on their argument, I headed around to the back, hoping that Bam's dumb ass hadn't run off with my money. The knob was locked, but I was able to push the door open since it wasn't closed all the way, and the second I stepped inside, my nose was attacked by a rancid smell. I pulled my shirt up over my nose and proceeded through his filthy ass kitchen, stopping short at the sight of a body lying in the middle of the floor just past the hallway. I approached while cursing under my breath, careful not to step too close. Bam had a single shot in the middle of his forehead, and his eyes were fixed on the ceiling. This was the second damn body I'd come in contact with in the last hour, and I couldn't help feeling like this was a bad omen. My search for my drugs or any of the money he should've had, was in vain. Whoever had gotten to him had taken it all and the nigga's phone too. For the second time that day, I left empty-handed and feeling like my back was against the wall. With no other plan to fall back on, I dialed the one number I knew I could get some type of help from.

DESTINY

*O*ur court date had approached quickly as hell, and I was so nervous that I was shaking as I got dressed. Even though, I knew that Antonio didn't have a chance in hell of being a better parent than me, I also knew that my recent record wouldn't look so good. Thankfully, the lawyer had handled the investigation regarding Dre's fake disappearance, so I no longer had that hanging over my head, but that didn't stop me from worrying. In my bra and panties, I walked back and forth to the closet laying different things out on the bed since I couldn't decide. So far, I had five outfits laid out and was heading back for a sixth when Juice entered the room, looking as cool as a cucumber.

"What you doin in here, shorty? Court start in like an hour and a half." He glanced down at the time on his AP before taking in all of the clothes on our bed.

"I knowww, I just can't find nothing that looks appropriate, and it's making me anxious as hell." I sighed in frustration.

"Shit, I see five things you can wear right here." His brows dipped. "You stressing for nothin, baby, you got this shit in the bag." Butterflies filled my stomach as he pulled me into him and kissed my pouting lips. It was like he always had an encouraging word for me. He had enough confidence for the both of us, and it did help a little.

"I just don't want nothing to go wrong. He been pulling so much fuck shit, it's no tellin what he got up his sleeve, today," I grumbled, but Juice only smirked knowingly.

"That nigga ain't got shit; I can promise you that. What you need to relax you, huh? Want me to eat this pussy right quick" My clit thumped involuntarily like he was speaking directly to it and chuckled at the silly look on his face.

"You play too much." Shaking my head, I made a weak attempt to wiggle out of his arms, but he only held me to him.

"Shiiit, who playing? I'm dead ass serious! You gone have my baby poppin out with gray hair with all the worrying you doin. If some head will calm yo ass down, then I'm gone eat that shit til you climbing the walls round this muhfucka!" I couldn't help but zero in on his juicy ass lips, and he licked them just to further entice me, grinning at how he was physically affecting my horny ass. It definitely did the trick though because I was no longer worrying about what Antonio was going to do in court, as visions of Juice's head between my legs filled my mind. He didn't wait for me to give him an answer; within seconds, he had my panties down and around my ankles.

"Juiiice!" I squealed as he scooped me up off my feet and sat me down on the dresser.

"You was ready, huh? You so damn wet, it's a puddle under you." He knew I liked that dirty talking. It was almost enough to make me cum without him even touching me.

"Ooooh mmmm." He ran his tongue up my center, damn near covering my whole pussy with his mouth, slurping loudly. I was glad that Yo'Sahn had decided to stay with Dream and Eazy the night before because the way Juice had me hitting high notes, my son would've thought I was being killed in here. He alternated between sucking and flicking his tongue rapidly, adding two fingers that he hooked upward, almost beckoning my orgasm.

"Mmm hmm, feed me that good shit, shorty," he ordered with a grunt. I ground my pussy against his face as I felt myself reaching my peak.

"Ohhhh fuck I- I'm cumming, Juice!" I was clawing at anything I could get my hands on, and my thighs clenched tightly as I came hard, soaking Juice's beard and the dresser. If he wasn't holding me up, my big ass would've fallen from how severe my body shook. I was still recovering when he stood to his feet with a pleased grin covering his face. My juices glistened all in his facial hair, and he wiped what he could away before helping me down on wobbly legs. He was so freaky that eating my pussy had his hard dick visible in the dress pants he wore.

"Feel better?" I couldn't even speak yet, so I just nodded my head, breathing heavily. "Good, come on let's get cleaned up." He kissed me deeply and smacked my bare ass. I watched him walk into the bathroom, stuck and thinking about how lucky I was to have his fine ass.

An hour later, we were walking into the courthouse hand-in-hand, and a bitch was much more calmed down. In fact, I was damn near floating and walking with an extra pep in my step, which probably had to do with Juice telling me that after court, we were going to finish what we started. Dream and Eazy, who'd been sitting outside of the courtroom, both came over at the sight of us.

"Bitch, you was pushin it. Five more minutes, and yo ass was gonna be late to your own hearing," Dream scolded as soon as she stood next to me.

"I know, I couldn't find nothing to wear, and I was nervous as hell. Juice got me right though, but how do I look?" I'd decided on a black and white, striped dress that stopped at my knees, with a black blazer and some high heels. My hair was bone straight with a part down the middle and simple diamond stud earrings. Besides my lashes and lipstick, my face was bare of makeup, but I wasn't trying to do too much.

"Y'all nasty asses." She smirked, bumping me lightly with her hip and then rubbing my belly. "You look beautiful though, boo. Don't even worry about Antonio's deadbeat ass. He ain't even made it yet." I wasn't surprised that he was running late. As much as he claimed to want his son, he still wasn't even able to get his shit together and show up on time. We both rolled our eyes heavenward, thinking the same thing I'm sure.

"I swear, he really just probably wasted all our time, but as long as we get this shit figured out, I don't even care. Hopefully, the judge will see through this weak ass attempt and just throw this shit out, today," I said lowly, glancing at Juice and Eazy, who stood a little bit away from us.

"Exactly, I'm really mad they even letting it get this far." Dream knew better than anybody about the tumultuous relationship between Antonio and me and how inactive he'd been in Yo'Sahn's life. It was crazy that they had let him do all of this after years of no interest in our son. Yoshi was literally a month away from his thirteenth birthday, and the man hadn't been involved consistently since he was a toddler.

Shaking my head at the stupidity of it all, I released a sigh. "Where's Yoshi at anyway?" I looked around for him in the wide hall.

"Oh, he went to the bathroom." She chuckled. "I told his ass not to eat no White Castle last night, but he don't listen. He been on the toilet all morning." Just as she said it, he emerged from around the corner, holding his stomach with a frown on his handsome face.

I'd had him pack his light blue button-up, dark blue slacks and a matching tie before he left and despite his scowl, he looked nice until I got down to his shoes and realized that he'd opted to wear his all-white Air Force Ones. When he saw us, he gave a weak smile and hurried over, and I had to refrain from slapping him upside the head. It definitely wouldn't look good at our first custody hearing if I put hands on him, but the look on my face let him know I wasn't pleased. I waited while he greeted Juice before going in on him.

"Boy, you know damn well you wasn't supposed to wear them gym shoes with that. You lucky we in this courthouse or I'd go upside yo head," I fussed with a hand on my hip.

"Maaa, them other shoes hurt my feet, and they sound like some girl shoes when I walk."

"Let my lil homie rock, he looks aight," Juice interjected before I could say anything else, gaining an appreciative look from Yo'Sahn. They dapped each other up, and I rolled my eyes because they were always trying to gang up on me. I could only imagine what it'd be like with another boy running around, but I still didn't want a girl.

"Fine, it's too late to do anything about it now anyway."

"Right, so calm yo lil bossy ass down," Juice told me, placing his hand in mine and pecking my lips quickly, just as our case was called. We all shuffled into the courtroom and took our seats, even though there was still no sign of Antonio.

The lawyer that Juice hired filled us in quickly about what would be happening, today, before the judge entered and called us to the front. I purposefully left Yo'Sahn sitting with Dream and walked to the podium with only Juice and our lawyer, Pruitt. She was clearly a beast when it came to family court and walked with confidence like there wasn't shot to worry about, which made me even more comfortable.

"Where is the other parent?" the judge asked no one in particular, and Pruitt jumped right in.

"Your Honor, since the plaintiff has obviously displayed a lack of concern in this case, I move that this matter be dismissed—" She was interrupted by the doors behind us being pushed open loudly, only for Antonio, his girlfriend, and his mama to walk through. I was immediately thrown by his appearance since he looked like he'd gotten his ass beat on the way here. The nigga's face was bruised, and he was sporting a busted lip. Not only that, but he was slightly limping and getting help to come down the aisle by his girlfriend. I heard Juice snicker behind me, but I couldn't even tear my eyes away from the mess I was seeing.

"Mr. Montgomery, is there a reason why you out just now entering my courtroom, fifteen minutes late?" the judge immediately dug in his ass as they settled behind their podium.

"No, ma'am. I apologize for my lateness," he cleared his throat and said.

"Well, are you alright to be here? You look awful, do you need us to reschedule at this time?" she asked, taking in how fucked-up he looked, despite his nice clothes.

"Uh, actually, Your Honor, I would like to drop the case completely. Destiny has been doing a great job with Yo'Sahn, and right now, I'm not in the position to take him fulltime or even part-time, to be honest."

My jaw dropped at his statement, and I had to look to see if it was really him talking. After raising all of the drama that he had, I was shocked that he'd even speak so highly of me once we got to court. The judge and everyone else in the courtroom's expression mirrored my own, obviously just as surprised as me.

"Excuse me? Are you saying that you no longer want to move forward with this case?" Disbelief was evident in her tone as she glared down at him over the rim of her glasses. Antonio glanced over to where I stood before nodding firmly.

"Yes, ma'am, that's exactly what I'm saying."

The judge regarded him for what felt like minutes as the room fell silent. Her heated gaze was almost that of a scolding parent. "Ms. Pruitt, does your client agree with this?" she asked with her eyes still on Antonio.

"Yes, she does, Your Honor," Pruitt said without hesitation.

"Well, this is certainly unexpected," she bristled, shuffling through papers before her. "Since you believe that the best place for the boy is with his mother and have no objection to her continuing to solely provide for him, then I will grant your request, however, I do recommend that you involve yourself in your son's life by way of visitation, at the discretion of the mother. I hope that your new feelings toward his placement is because you truly believe it's in his best interest and not because you've been coerced."

"No, ma'am, I really do think he's in good hands with his mama," Antonio let her know quickly.

She started talking again, but at this point, I wasn't paying any attention to her. My eyes were on Juice, who was looking straight ahead like he didn't feel me staring a hole in his face. Honestly, the thought hadn't crossed my mind that he would've been responsible for the way Antonio looked, but now that she'd said something, it all made sense. All of the smart-ass remarks that he'd made, and his extra confidence was because he knew he'd beat the man's ass.

The judge banged her gavel and brought me out of my thoughts as a chorus of cheers erupted around us. I allowed Juice to pull me into a hug, while Pruitt congratulated us both. By the time he released me, Antonio and his family was gone, and Yoshi was already happily running my way. After hugging my baby and sister, we headed out with him tucked under my arm.

"Let's go celebrate! IHOP, on me!" Eazy said as soon as we were outside. The mention of food had my stomach growling. I hadn't wanted to eat much before leaving home, but Juice had made me eat a bag of mini muffins, and now, my baby was ready for something real.

"Bet, you know I love a free meal." Juice nodded and rubbed his hands together. "Text me which one we meeting at. Come on, bae." He was already pulling me in the direction of the car with Yo'Sahn bouncing alongside us.

I wanted to ask him if he'd made Antonio say that shit in court, but something was telling me I didn't even need to. This was proven further when he brought my hand up to his lips and winked at me while we drove. With a sexy smirk and a shrug, he mouthed, "Told you." I couldn't even be mad at him. Just like he'd said, he took care of things and had me feeling all warm and fuzzy inside. I swear, it was nothing better than a man that came through by any means necessary. As mean as he was, Juice always found a way to show me he cared. Once again, I found myself thanking God for his rude ass and wanting to suck his dick at the same time.

DREAM

oday was Destiny's gender reveal, and I was running around getting last-minute things ready for her. With the help of Elijah and Mr. King, I'd been able to pull everything off while still running the salon, and I couldn't wait for her to see it. Since her court date, she'd been in a good ass mood, and as far as I knew, hadn't heard anything else from Antonio's bitch ass. Elijah told me all about Juice fucking him up, and it served him right. I could have understood if he was trying to see Yoshi or get visitation but even then, it was no reason to get the courts or DCFS involved. In my opinion, he deserved that ass-whooping plus some.

Popping the trunk on my brand-new Audi, I grabbed as many bags as I could and turned around, running straight into Elijah. Disapproval was written all over his face as he relieved me of each bag.

"I could've carried those," I huffed after he gave me a quick kiss and went to get the rest of the stuff from the trunk.

"But I'm right here, so it ain't no need," he said when the last of the bags were in his hands. He waited while I closed the trunk back up before following me inside of the building.

"You can sit that stuff right over here." I pointed to the empty table that I'd planned to set the snacks on. I'd put everything together the night before, so all I'd have to do was set it up. Everything was pink and blue in honor of Baby King. There were bags of pink and blue cotton candy, specially made M&Ms, suckers, gum balls, cookies, and any type of candy you could imagine. The room was also decorated in pink and blue balloons and streamers with a special throne set up for Juice and Destiny, with blocks on each side that read boy on her side and girl on his. Games were set up in the back towards the deck and each table had a tiny blue or pink block with balloons tied to them. It had taken me a week to get the decorations done with the assistance of a few of the girls from the shop, and I was extremely pleased with the way it had turned out.

"Damn, you hooked this place up, it looks good as hell." Elijah came up from behind and wrapped his arms around me as he took in the room. Even though I knew I'd done a good job, it felt good to hear him say it too, and I couldn't help but beam happily.

"Thanks, I just hope Destiny likes it." I giggled, knowing that despite her recent good mood, she'd probably be anxious and snappy today.

"She gone love it, and you got all this junk food here. Yeah, her greedy ass gone be in heaven."

"Don't be talkin bout my sister!" I elbowed him in his side with a laugh. We all knew how she was over food, at this point, and pretty much if anything edible was in the vicinity, then she'd be cool. That didn't mean he could say it though.

"Shit, I'm just stating facts, nephew got her ass eatin up everything." Unlike his brother and Yoshi, Elijah was dead set on the baby being a boy, and he was rocking a powder blue polo shirt to show it. As part of the gender reveal theme, I requested that everyone wear a color to represent their guess of the baby's sex. Since I only wanted he or she to be healthy, I was wearing a sundress with both pink and blue.

"I'm telling her, you said that shit too," I feigned anger and wiggled away from him and over to set up the table.

"Ain't nobody scared of Destiny's ass! All I gotta do is get Juice, and she gone pipe down," he lied, only making me shake my head.

"You just making it worse cause I'm telling her that too."

"Mannn, come here." He snatched me up and turned my body, so that I was facing him. The look on his face had my pussy tingling instantly, but I pushed him away, already knowing that he'd definitely have me bent over one of these tables.

"Stop, Elijah cause I already know what that look means." I playfully rolled my eyes while he smirked and slipped his arms back around me.

"What it mean?" His voice was muffled as he buried his face into my neck, planting soft kisses there. He knew exactly what he was doing. My knees became weak and a soft moan slipped from my lips. "You know it ain't shit to just lift this dress up, right?"

"Ahem!"

We both looked up to see a delivery man, standing in the doorway and sent up a silent thank you to God because I was damn sure about to let Elijah take me right there at my sister's party. I moved away from a grinning Elijah and smiled, slightly embarrassed.

"Hi, I'm sorry about that," I quickly apologized as I approached the man, who had an amused look on his face.

"No need to apologize, young lady, me and my wife are the same way. It's always good to see black love," he told me with a wink that had me blushing. "I got your cake here. Are you Miss Dream Parker?"

I couldn't even hide my smile as he looked down at the clipboard he was holding and back up at me. "Yep, that's me." I accepted the pen from him and scribbled my signature excitedly.

Super Sweets was one of the newest businesses to pop-up in Chicago, and after seeing their business page on Instagram, I just knew they had to make Destiny's cake. The lady had shown me a few different ideas, but when I saw the piñata cake with a baby leaning over into a gift box, I knew it was the one. I had her add *"Little Sister or Little Brother"* on it to include Yoshi into the festivities, and I was excited to see it. He'd been through so much and was still such a sweetheart. I knew a lot of that had to do with having Juice and Eazy around.

"Alright, I'll be right back with the cake," the man said, snapping me out of my thoughts. I waited anxiously while he brought it in and set the box on the table with Elijah's assistance. Once he left, and I finally got the table set up to my liking, I stood back and admired my hard work. Everything looked so good.

In no time, the food arrived, and the guests started pouring in, all marveling at the decorations. I wasn't even surprised by how many ended up wearing blue in hopes that the baby would be a boy. Juice's rough ass was definitely meant to father a son, I just didn't know if we were all ready to have a little him running around. I bounced from one side of the room to the other, making sure things were in place and everybody was having a good time since Destiny was due to arrive shortly. Nobody had a clue what the actual sex was, and it had been hard as hell to keep it a secret from Elijah, who had been going out of his way to get it out of me.

I caught his eye just as one of their aunts cornered me and damn near melted. When I say that things had been nothing short of amazing between us, that was no exaggeration. He'd been showing and proving since I'd decided to give him another chance, and I hadn't regretted it yet. I could barely focus on whatever his aunty was saying as I followed the movement of his tongue across his bottom lip. It was like my body was so in tuned with him that my clit was already thumping. Thank God Destiny chose that moment to arrive or else, I would've been pulling his fine ass into the bathroom.

"Awww!" She was already tearing up as everyone began clapping.

She looked gorgeous in a baby blue fitted skirt that flowed at the feet and a cute pink baby tee that tied on top of her belly. Her natural hair was still straitened and was in a half-up, half-down style with a bun on top and the rest flowing down past her shoulders. A light beat had her glowing, or it may have just been the pregnancy because it had been very good to her. She hid her face in Juice's chest, gaining a chorus of awwws from everyone. Juice just wrapped his arms around her affectionately, even as his smart-ass talked shit.

"Cut all that soft ass crying out," he prodded, looking just as fresh as she did.

His lining was fresh and the pink button-up and light wash jeans looked surprisingly good with the white blazer he had on. Yoshi emerged behind them, wearing the exact same thing, and I made a mental note to get a picture of them all together before the party ended.

"Man, Juice, what you do already?" was the first thing out of his mouth when he saw the state his mama was in. We all chuckled at the scowl on his handsome face. He too had obviously been to the barber shop, judging from his hairline and how fresh his dreads looked.

"I ain't do it! Her cry baby ass started as soon as we got in here!" Juice defended with a frown.

"Oh snap, ma, you trippin!" They laughed together at her expense.

"See, let me get my sister something to eat cause y'all already got her messed-up!" I swatted at them both, but at the mention of food, Destiny's head popped up, and she quickly dabbed her tears away.

"You got some fries with mild sauce?" She looked at me with a sniffle, and I had to laugh myself. Just like that, she was okay. Shaking my head, I gave them all a quick hug and led her through the crowded room where she greeted her guests until we got to the food. She promptly piled her plate high and then went to sit in her designated seat.

An hour later, we had played all of the games and given away the prizes. Destiny had eaten and danced the time away, and it felt so good to see her in her glow. After years of watching her struggle in her relationships, she seemed genuinely happy and despite Juice's rough around the edges ass, I loved seeing them together.

"Alright, it's the moment you all been waiting for!" I announced, drawing everyone's attention. "If you'll all meet me out on the deck, we're gonna find out what we're having!"

"Awwww, yeah! It's that time!" Juice was flashing all thirty-two of his teeth and rubbing his hands together like Birdman, instantly gaining a playful groan from Destiny. Jumping to his feet, he helped her out of the chair she was in, and they made their way outside behind everyone else.

I had searched for the perfect way for them to reveal the baby's sex, wanting it to be different but just as fun as all of the other ones, I'd seen on Pinterest and Facebook. Everybody and their mama had done the confetti balloons and the smoke sticks, and I wanted her reveal to be one of a kind and incorporate their personalities too. It didn't take long for me to come up with the perfect way to announce their little bundle.

"You ready for this?" I grinned sneakily as I sat the small box down and prepared to open it.

"Stop playing, Dream, so I can prove yo sister wrong," Juice cracked, and Destiny slapped his arm playfully.

"Ain't nobody gone be wrong but yo ass," she huffed before

her brows dipped when I opened the box and held out two cap guns to them. "What the hell?"

"You're a firecracker, and he's a wild one, so I figured we might as well find out with a bang." Shrugging, I handed Yo'Sahn the last gun that I had, so he could get in on the fun too. "Okay, y'all on the count of three!"

"One, two, three!"

Bang! Bang! Bang!

They set their guns off, and the crowd erupted in cheers as pink smoke filled the air, letting everyone know it was a girl. Destiny started crying again, but the smile on her face told me they were happy tears as Juice and Yoshi jumped around and slapped each other a five.

"I told yo ass!" he said happily as he grabbed her up into a hug and grinded against her. "Daddy know what I'm doin."

"Ugh man, get up off my mama!"

Yoshi had a hard time pulling off a disgruntled face because he was smiling so widely. He eased up on the other side of her and gave her a hug and kiss before Juice shocked the hell out of us all and dropped down to one knee. We all went wild and geared up to record and snap pictures, even though I'd hired a professional videographer and photographer. Once we all quieted down, Juice grabbed ahold of my sister's hand and pulled out the fattest ring I'd ever seen.

"Juiiice, oh my God!" Destiny gasped through her tears.

"I ain't never thought there'd be a day when I'd be satisfied with just one woman, but ever since I met yo aggy ass, I've done things I swore I never would. You changed my life for the better and made me a better man. Shit, you even gave me a son and now a daughter, so it's only right that I give you something…. You already have my heart, now I just need you to take my last name. Will you marry me?" My vision was blurry from the ugly cry I was doing as we all waited for Destiny to answer.

"Awww, babe, yesss!"

He slipped the ring on her finger, and they embraced as we all gathered around them. Mr. King was one of the first to reach them and offer his congratulations with pride all over his face. I know Ms. Rachel has to be smiling down from heaven, and I wished she would've been here. She'd be just as proud. When I finally made it close enough, I gave my sister a hug. Our lives were just getting better and better, and I couldn't wait to see what else the future held for us.

JUICE

Man, after proposing to Destiny, a nigga had been on cloud nine. I had my girl, my son, and we were going to be bringing my baby girl into the world soon. The only thing hanging over our heads was the fact that we still hadn't gotten at Budda. We had him boxed in, though, so it wouldn't be much longer. Hopefully, it'd be over tonight. After killing off his little crew, he had no one to turn to, but we still had one trick left up our sleeves.

"What up ninety-day fiancée?" Eazy joked, dapping me up as he jumped in the car with me.

He'd been making little funny comments ever since the gender reveal, but I knew his ass was proud of the direction I was headed in. I'd had a serious conversation with him and Pops before I even got the ring, and he'd already told me it was a good look. He was just tryna be funny even though everybody knows I'm the funny one.

"Shit, I had to do something. You been on yo Keith Sweat begging shit, making me look bad."

"Nigga, fuck you!" He laughed cause he knew I was telling

the truth. This nigga was one step away from writing poetry to express his feelings for her on some Love Jones shit.

"Aye, it ain't my fault you out here on yo romance movie shit. You probably got a ring ready yo damn self and just scared she gone tell yo ass no." I was cracking up, but when I noticed how quiet he was, I shot a questioning look his way. "Ohhhh damnnnn, you do?" The sour ass expression on his face gave me my answer before he could speak, and I damn near choked on the weed I was smoking.

"Dream definitely gone say yes if I ask. I'm just tryna let y'all have y'all moment." He shrugged, sounding more confident than he looked. I knew the day would come when he took his head out of his ass and tried to make things right with Dream. If Trell was here, we would've been making bets on whether or not she took him back, and I would have been the one betting she did. When he forced his way in her crib after getting shot, I just knew she was going to torture him every chance she got, but I'd been wrong, and it seemed like that time had only brought them closer. Him buying another shop and putting Sherice in her place had probably played a major role in their reunion too, but it was obvious that Dream still loved the nigga's dirty draws.

"Don't wait on my account. Me and Destiny good, shit we got a lot going on. She already planning it for after she have the baby and get her body back, anyway. Her words, not mine," I told him truthfully. We'd had a long conversation after the gender reveal with Yo'Sahn too, even though I'd already asked for his blessing. Waiting awhile to actually jump the broom was cool with me; I was down for whatever she wanted.

He mumbled, "Bet," seemingly done with the conversation and sat up higher in his seat as we pulled up alongside Pierre's car at the warehouse. "What he doin here?"

"He want in." I shrugged, dumping my ashes out of the window and taking a pull before handing the blunt to him.

"Bruh, he need to sit his old ass down."

"Pops need a life too, Jody!" Cackling, I climbed out behind him after he shot me an annoyed look. After Pierre pulled that "Fatal Attraction" shit and came to Eazy's club with the info on Budda, Eazy wasn't as hostile with him. I'd never understood what his buff ass was so mad about in the first place. Sure, they had lied his whole life, but it wasn't like it was to hurt him, and honestly, it hadn't been a bad life. Since I'd been around Destiny and Yo'Sahn, I'd come to realize a lot about raising kids. It's hard to see it as the child in the situation, but parents are only human. And some parents, the good ones anyway, they make decisions based on what they feel is best.

There'd been plenty of times I saw Destiny piss Yo'Sahn off by either making him do something or denying him something. It wasn't ever to intentionally harm him, although I'm sure in the moment that's how he felt, it was just to better him, and that's why I think Pierre had decided to step away. I think Eazy was finally starting to see that for himself. Pops, on the other hand, was a whole different issue. His old ass didn't see it for Pierre at all, and it had more to do with their own shit. I know I'd want to kill a muthafucka that felt the same way about Destiny that I did, but that was just me though.

We pulled back the door to the warehouse and stepped inside to see Pierre's goons going to work on Santos' while he sat in a chair, puffing on a cigar. Judging from his rolled-up sleeves and the dried blood decorating his knuckles, he'd had a hand in the beating too.

"Damn, Pierre, we need the nigga to be able to talk," I told him, eyeing Santos' mangled body. They'd obviously been fucking him up for a while. He looked close to death, but that could've been how much blood he had covering him. I couldn't even see the man's face to tell who it was, the only reason I knew was because we'd brought him here.

Chuckling, Pierre motioned for his men to stop their assault. "We got a little carried away while we waited on Budda's call, but he should be able to speak just fine," he assured me and stood to his feet. His eyes gleamed as he strolled over to where Santos sat, moaning.

"This nigga," Eazy grumbled, shaking his head as we watched him crouch down.

"What you gone say when that muhfucka call back, San?"

Santos' head rolled back, and he groaned from the movement, but he still struggled through what he was supposed to say. "Tt-to meet me....at the res-taurant."

"Good, next time, don't stutter so much. You understand that this is what happens when you fuck with my blood? You *never* fuck with what's mine." Pierre blew smoke in his face and turned back towards us with a smirk. "See, talking perfectly." Despite his antics, I thought the nigga was boss as fuck, and I couldn't help my own grin. He was in here Gucci'd down in some Ferragamo shoes and an AP, beating a nigga bloody. I'd never seen a muhfucka handle some shit like this in a suit. I made a mental note to try it one day.

Eazy checked his watch. "What time he supposed to be callin?" he asked, looking bored in comparison to me.

"Eleven, so in about twenty minutes," Pierre said over his shoulder as he slapped Santos to rouse him back awake.

I took my ass to find a seat, so I could save my energy. After all of the mayhem that Budda had caused, it was his ass I wanted to fuck up. I wasn't wasting a bruised knuckle on Santos. Eazy must have been on the same time as me because he propped himself up on one of the many tables in the room. I was surprised when Pierre went over and started asking him about him and Dream's situation, which had me thinking that he'd talked to him about her at some point. I guess, he wanted as many opinions as he could get, but as far as I could see, they were in a much better place than they were even a month ago. My phone vibrated in my pocket, and Destiny's smiling face popped up on my screen.

"Didn't I just leave yo whiny ass?" I quizzed, even though I was smiling just as wide as she was. She instantly rolled her eyes and blew out an irritated breath.

"I just wanted to let you know, I love you, and I put you up another plate for later."

My grin grew at her being considerate as she batted them long ass butterfly lashes at me. "I love yo ass too, but what you want, bruh, cause you could've just texted me that."

"See, you always gotta ruin some shit," she huffed with a pout. "I was just tryna be nice to yo bop head ass."

"Oh, ayite then, I'll be back in a minute." Without waiting on her to reply, I hung up and counted down from three, knowing that she was gone call me right back and just like clockwork, my phone went off again.

"Why you hang up on me, nigga!" She was now laying down on her back in bed, and I could see the top of her cleavage coming out of her bra, instantly making my mouth water. Destiny was always stacked, but my baby girl had her thicker than cold grits and her titties damn near two sizes bigger.

"Shit, you said you was just callin to say you loved me and you put me up a plate, I thought you was done." I held in a laugh at how her perfectly arched brows furrowed. "You wanted something else?"

"You so full of shit, Juice, you know I wanted something else!" Her whiny ass voice had my dick coming alive because she sounded the exact same when I was deep in them guts. Almost everything she did these days had me ready to fuck; my attraction to her had grown tenfold. It was from a mixture of her carrying my seed and how much my love had grown for her.

Licking my lips, I lowered my voice some, so only she could hear. "Nah, I'm just fuckin with you. What you want, baby?" She already knew what I was on just from the look in my eyes, and I knew she was clenching them thighs together.

"Juiiiice, don't do that," she cooed sexily, and I chuckled.

"I ain't even do shit, I'm asking what you want," I lied.

She rolled her eyes again before rattling off a long ass list of snacks she wanted me to bring home. I smirked, knowing that was the whole reason she'd even called, but I didn't even say shit. I just put everything she asked for in my mental rolodex before we said our goodbyes. Stuffing my phone down into pocket, I looked up to see all eyes on me and my lip curled at the look on their faces. "Fuck y'all lookin at?"

"Nothin." Eazy shook his head with a sneaky grin while everyone else just looked away. Thankfully, Santos' phone rang right then. Pierre hopped up from his spot beside Eazy, rubbing his hands together with that damn cigar still hanging between his lips.

"Showtime muhfucka!" he spoke, slapping Santos, who was still barely conscious as one of the men with him held the phone up to the man's ear. "Say *exactly* what you're supposed to."

With the phone on speaker, we all heard Budda's voice come through loud and clear. "Hello? Santos you there?" It had been a minute since I'd heard that nigga's voice but there was no mistaking it was him, and as expected, he sounded scared as hell. We'd flushed out his back up, and the only person he had left was Santos, but we had him.

"Ye-yeah?" he stuttered, and Pierre gave him a murderous look.

"Look, you said to call you back later."

"I was handling business earlier," Santos spoke slowly in an attempt to regulate his voice, but the nigga was still panting like he'd run a marathon. "But I can meet you at the restaurant in thirty."

"I hope yo old ass not getting some pussy when I'm callin you for help, man!" Budda's stress was evident as he commented on Santos' speech.

"Don't worry about what I'm doin. Are you stopping by or

what?" We all waited impatiently for the nigga to say he was coming.

"I'll be there."

Pierre motioned for his guy to hang up the phone before turning to us. "Y'all niggas ready?"

EAZY

*I*t was finally time to get this shit over with, and I had mixed feelings. Having my mentor be the one raising all this hell over the past few months was a hard pill to swallow, but he certainly deserved death for all of his misdeeds. I didn't have any sympathy for his ass, I just knew that he needed to suffer. There was no way I could allow his shit to be quick and painless. Not after killing Trell and being behind my mama's death. I wanted to carry the shit out for days if I could, but I knew that wasn't happening. He'd been fucking with the Feds, and I didn't know whether or not they'd be looking for him. Or worse, come at us because of his disappearance.

We rode to the restaurant with Santos in the trunk of a beater while Pierre's men, whose names I still didn't know, drove his truck. Without knowing whether or not Budda was already there scoping the front, we felt it would be best if we had Santos car parked in its usual spot while we went in around the back.

Walking behind a limping Santos, I pulled my gloves down tighter and checked my gun. Pierre was to my left and Juice was on the right, both brimming with excitement that was evident in their faces. Pierre because it had been so long since he'd actually put in work like this and Juice because he was always happy to put a nigga to rest. Me, on the other hand, I held my composure much better, but I could feel my adrenaline rushing. Budda was a bitch, he was just good at hiding, so it wouldn't take much to get him down. Now, there wasn't anywhere left for him to hide. He was all out of options.

As soon as we got into the office, Juice pushed Santos down into his chair and took a seat on the corner of the desk in front of him. Relief washed over the older man's face from being off of his feet, but I was sure it wouldn't last long. A knock sounded at the door, and Budda was shoved inside. His eyes widened at a bloody Santos and Juice next to him, before he focused on me and tried to scramble out of the room. If the situation wasn't so serious, I'd have laughed at the cartoonish looking attempt.

"Don't run, nigga." Juice smirked in a teasing tone, after I'd pulled him back away from the door by his neck.

I could've easily snapped his shit from the rage that erupted in me after getting my hands on him. I'd been calm and cool so far, but with the nigga this close, I could no longer control myself. He gasped and clawed at his neck as my grip tightened, trying to cut off any air to his body. Juice was still sitting there, watching in pleasure as Budda's body dropped to the floor.

"Hurry and tie this nigga up," I panted, trying to calm myself back down.

I'd come really close to actually killing that nigga right then, but I'd stopped short, merely putting him to sleep. As pissed as I was, I didn't want to ruin our plans by having him meet his end here. After his hands and feet were secured, Pierre had his men come back and carry him to the car.

"Ok, you got what you wanted. Let me go now, I don't have nothing to do with this," Santos started begging as soon as he was gone, and Pierre made his way behind his chair.

"See that's where you're wrong." Pierre pinned him down

with one hand on his shoulder and his gun in the other just as the door came open again and his son, Manuel, walked in pointing his own gun.

"What are you doin, *mijo?*" Santos' eyes bounced wildly around the room, and he struggled to get out of Pierre's hold to no avail.

"I told you that messing with that *rato!* You leave me no choice, you're obviously not in your right state of mind. So, it's time I take over." Manuel shrugged coldly, firing two shots into his father's chest, killing him before he could respond.

"That was some straight up telemundo shit!" Juice cracked, causing Manuel to shoot an evil look his way. "Fuck you lookin at me like that for? You the one killed yo own pops, nigga!"

"It needed to be done! He was fuckin up!"

"Whatever, help you sleep at night," Juice grumbled with a doubtful mug.

"Well, either way our business here is complete. You now have reign over your father's empire," Pierre cut in, stopping the ensuing argument. "Do you need help getting this shit cleaned up?"

Manuel looked around the room and shook his head, before telling us that he could handle it. He'd turned on his own father for his crown and access to better product and didn't seem to feel any remorse. That wasn't my business though. What he did with the shit was on him and Pierre.

"Okay, cool." Pierre started to leave the room but turned at the last minute like he had another thought. "You do know that I'll kill you if you fuck up, right?" He squinted over at Manuel, who seemed shook up by the question.

"Ye-yeah," he stammered, nodding stupidly.

"Well, alright then." Smirking, Pierre left the room the same way we'd come, leaving both me and Juice confused and probably Manuel too. It wasn't until we made it outside and to the car that I realized why the nigga was being all cryptic and shit.

We'd barely pulled out of the alley when an explosion sounded that rocked the whole block.

"Damnnnn! The fuck was that!" Juice went off in the back-seat, looking out of the window behind us. From the rearview, I could see the fire coming from the building and raised an eyebrow up at Pierre, who was sitting in the passenger seat unbothered.

"What? I know you ain't think I was bouta trust that nigga? I'm a lil old, but I ain't crazy." I couldn't even do shit but shake my head at his ass. He'd made the deal with Manuel just to kill him in the end. I had to admit that it did seem stupid to work with a snake that would set up his own daddy. I guess, he wasn't smarter than his pops after all.

Not even an hour later, we were back at the warehouse, and Budda was finally coming to after being knocked out again upon our arrival. I smirked as he woke up, looking around before his gaze landed on me. "Welcome back, lil bitch."

He struggled against his restraints. "You think you doin somethin, nigga, I made you! You wouldn't be shit without me!" His outburst had me and Juice laughing. I couldn't even believe that at one time I looked up to this nigga.

"Gone head and get yo lil villain speech out, now cause in a minute you ain't gone be able to say shit."

"Suck my dick! Even with me dead the Feds still comin for you! So, enjoy yo freedom while you still can, nigga!" he spat angrily.

"This nigga really had a speech though! I'm fuckin dead!" Juice's immature ass chuckled over his head, only adding to the humor of his idle threats. Unfazed, I bent down closer and flashed a quick grin.

"I'll make sure to keep that in mind," I snickered. Standing to my full height, I reared back and kicked the shit out of him, sending his ass into the four-foot hole I'd had dug out. Budda was still trying to act hard, but his tough act was short-lived when I lifted the bottle of acid and began pouring it over his body, starting with his feet. Immediately, he was howling in pain as it ate through his skin and smoke starting wafting out. I took my time going over each leg and up his torso, saving his head for last and watching in pleasure as the life left his body.

"That shit stink!" Juice fussed dramatically, waving his hand in front of his face and gagging. "Fuck happened to just shooting a muhfucka? You and this nigga doing all this psycho shit!" He pointed towards Pierre, who was sitting by quietly smoking another cigar. I swear, the nigga had one for each occasion.

"I think the punishment should fit the crime." Pierre shrugged, still as calm as a cucumber.

"Well, I think y'all muhfuckas need to leave me outta shit, unless it's some bullets involved!" Juice walked off grumbling, leaving just me and Pierre. He chuckled and came over to me.

"You feel better?"

My forehead bunched at the question. I couldn't say I felt *better* or even vindicated by Budda's death. I would've felt much better if my mama and Trell were alive, but at least I knew the nigga who was responsible, died by my hands and had suffered. He'd promised them on one of his many visits to their graves that he'd avenge them, and he had as best he could. "Shit, it is what it is. That nigga gone," was all I could manage to say, and he nodded in understanding. With him out of the way, I could move on finally and continue growing with Dream. The shit was finally over.

DESTINY

ONE YEAR LATER...

"*P*lease, put yo hands together and welcome Mr. and Mrs. Elijah Kinnnng!" the DJ announced the newly-weds and just like everyone else, I was shouting and clapping loudly.

After everything that had gone down, they'd finally worked out their issues and their love was just as strong as ever. I couldn't front, I'd had my doubts about whether or not they'd be able to rebuild their trust in each other, but even a blind person could see how much love they shared. Dream twerked against him as they entered the ballroom, making everybody erupt in laughter and egging them on.

"She better stop before she shake that baby loose!" Juice said loud enough for only me to hear. I nudged him with my elbow and looked around to make sure nobody heard him. Dream was about three months pregnant and was waiting to tell everybody until she was farther along when she was in the safe zone. He shot an irritated look my way, and I returned the gesture rolling my eyes.

"Aye, fat-fat, tell her to keep her hands to herself before I let you handle my light weight!" he told our daughter, who was looking just as mean as him at the moment.

Our beautiful daughter Ja'Miah had just turned eight months and was just as bad as any boy could've been. She was a straight up daddy's girl too, just like his ass had predicted. The only time she fucked with me was when she wanted to eat and when Juice wasn't around, but I loved her little chocolate self. Since she was starting to try and walk, Dream had put her in the wedding as the flower girl, and she'd looked so cute walking down the aisle holding her daddy's hand in her little puffy maroon dress and two pig tails with bows.

"Girl, I wish you would!" I told her, rolling my neck and sending her into a fit of baby talk that meant she was talking her shit. She killed me with her little petty self.

I could only hope that the baby that was growing inside of me at the moment was on my side. I'd just found out that Juice's ugly ass had trapped me with another baby that morning, and I was waiting until after the wedding to let him know. I already knew that he was going to be extra happy, and I had to admit that I was too. Being pregnant at the same time as my sister was going to be fun, and at least if I was out of commission, then we could do it together.

"Yup, cuss her ass out fat!" Juice egged her on, planting a kiss on her fat cheek.

I playfully rolled my eyes again and went to walk off, but he pulled me right back. "Awww, don't be jealous baby, daddy got kisses for you too," he teased in a baby voice and bent to kiss my pouting lips softly, making me melt all over. Of course, Ja'Miah started crying at the affection he was showing me with her cock-blocking ass.

"Man, what y'all doin to my sister? She ain't tryna see all that!" Yoshi walked up and chucked her up out of her father's arms, giving her a kiss and tickling her fat belly through her dress. Just that fast, she was laughing. She loved the hell out of her big brother and vice versa. They were already as thick as thieves, and he often had her when he wasn't in school, at basketball practice, or out somewhere. He walked off with her and blended into the crowd, no doubt taking her to get some snacks since he stayed feeding her goodies. With them gone, Juice wrapped his arms around me and cupped my ass like we weren't in a room full of people to which I quickly moved them back up.

"You looking good as fuck in this dress, girl, I might have to put another baby up in you," he growled in my ear, and I tried to hold back a grin but failed. We were both a part of the wedding party, so I too was wearing a tight-fitting mermaid, maroon gown, and he was wearing the hell out of his black suit with a maroon bow tie. He knew he was looking fine as hell too. I'd had to check a few hoes for looking too hard already.

"It's too late for that, baby daddy." I rubbed the back of his neck as I spoke, anticipating his excitement. At first, he squinted confused before his face lit up.

"Y-you already pregnant?"

I nodded anxiously, surprised by how happy I was to make him happy. These days, all I wanted was to see his fine ass smiling, and he was the same way. He was even starting to begin the steps to go legit like Eazy had, just so that he could make us proud. Every day, I tried to let him know that he'd more than exceeded my expectations, and I was blessed to have him.

"I already knew that shit, girl, I was just waiting on you to say something! Shit, it took you long enough, as many damn times as I poked holes in the condoms." His cocky ass shocked me, and I went to slap him.

"Nigga, what!"

"I'm jokin man, damn! I wasn't even really wearin that shit!"

"I can't stand yo ass, Juice!" I grumbled, even though I couldn't stop the laughter that bubbled in my throat. He was a straight asshole, but he was mine.

145

"I love you too!" he said cupping my chin and kissing me deeply. I couldn't even stay mad at him, and he knew it too. My whole life I'd been trying to find and keep love, and the minute I wasn't looking, I'd fucked around and low key fell for his savage ass, but I'd never been happier.

The End.

AN AMERICAN HUSTLER

Click the link to stay up to date: https://www.colehartsignature.com/an-american-hustler/

THANK YOU

Cole Hart
SIGNATURE NOVELS

To our loyal Cole Hart Signature readers,

Cole Hart Signature is always growing and changing. Some of you have been following Cole Hart since the beginning of his career, while others have seen us go from Cole Hart Presents to Cole Hart Signature. Then there are our daily new supporters who've only known us for what we are as a company today. Despite our changes, how or when you became a fanatic, we want to kindly thank you for the support.

We appreciate all our Cole Hart Readers because without every single one of you, we wouldn't be the company we are today.

If this book is your first introduction to our company, welcome! And be sure to sign up for email list by click the link, http://bit.ly/2BtGCXH, and joining out text-mail list by texting Cole-HartSig to (855)231-5230. Cole Hart Signature also has a Facebook group where fans get to discuss the plot, characters, overall releases about their favorite book. If itching for new and interesting conversation, click the link, https://geni.us/ ColeHartSignatureRead, to join today!

Lastly, Cole Hart Signature is always interested in partnering with aspiring authors, new or experienced, who thrive in the African Urban Fiction and Romance Fiction genre. If you're interested in joining our team, go to www. colehartsignature.com/submissions.

Once again, we truly appreciate all the support over the years.

Much Love,
   CHS

.

Made in the USA
Middletown, DE
20 February 2021